AIRBO

N

A World War 3 Technothriller Action Event

Dedication:

This book is for my beloved fiancé, Ebony.
-Nick.

About the Series:
The WW3 novels are a chillingly authentic collection of action-packed combat thrillers that envision a modern war where the world's superpowers battle on land, air and sea using today's military hardware.

Each title is a 50,000-word stand-alone adventure that forms part of an ever-expanding series, with several new titles published every year.

Facebook: https://www.facebook.com/NickRyanWW3
Website: https://www.worldwar3timeline.com
Cover design by: Other Worlds Design

Other titles in the collection:
- 'Charge to Battle'
- 'Enemy in Sight'
- 'Viper Mission'
- 'Fort Suicide'
- 'The Killing Ground'
- 'Search and Destroy'
- 'Airborne Assault'
- 'Defiant to the Death'
- 'A Time for Heroes'

The Invasion of Poland

For the first few savage weeks of the War in Europe, the Russian military machine seemed unstoppable. Within days of launching their attacks into the Baltic States, Lithuania, Latvia and Estonia had all been brutally conquered.

NATO troops that survived the furious onslaught were thrown back into Poland in disarray as ominous storm clouds gathered over the Suwalki Gap.

Allied commanders knew the narrow stretch of land between the Russian enclave of Kaliningrad, and the northwest corner of Belarus was a vulnerable corridor through which Russian troops could drive their Armies deep into Poland.

In the years prior to the outbreak of war, NATO forces had studied this vulnerable sixty-four mile long stretch of ground in minute detail, conducting joint training missions in the area on several occasions and concentrating forces in anticipation of the fateful day when war broke out.

The Russians, too, understood the strategic importance of seizing the Suwalki Gap. Taking control of the border would cut the Baltics off from NATO and open a corridor southwest to Warsaw and ultimately west to the German border.

When the first Russian tanks and APCs poured across the Lithuanian frontier into Poland, no one was surprised.

The Russian attack rolled southwest like an avalanche of steel behind a shattering bombardment of artillery. The NATO units in their way were quickly brushed aside as the invaders drove forward, turning the lush countryside into a war-ravaged wasteland.

NATO reacted quickly, moving its available forces in Poland northeast to block the enemy advance. Grimly, Allied commanders admitted that the Russian attack was more ferocious and more overwhelming than they had ever anticipated. Allied troops were stretched thread-bare and quickly overwhelmed by massed enemy firepower.

When Russian victory seemed inevitable, and with their Armies on the brink of breaking out into central Poland and thrusting towards Warsaw, a sudden second Axis attack threatened to completely collapse all Allied resistance.

The surprise attack came from the Belarusian 11th Guards Mechanized Brigade and plunged like a knife into the heart of Poland. Launched to coincide with the Russian attack through the Suwalki Gap, the Belarusian spearhead stormed across the Bug River at Brest and drove west.

The Allies were completely blindsided by the second enemy spearhead.

Standing in the Belarusian Army's way were just two companies of American paratroopers from the 173rd Airborne Brigade and a battalion of Polish troops who were conducting joint training exercises in the woods around the Polish city of Biala Podlaska.

It was a fight the handful of Allied troops could never hope to win against an overwhelming onslaught of enemy tanks and troops and artillery – unless they could hold out until help arrived.

But with Allied forces already stretched to breaking point to contain the Russian advance through the Suwalki Gap, NATO Commanders quickly realized there was only one possible way to relieve the beleaguered defenders…

An airborne assault.

BIALA PODLASKA TRAINING BASE
CENTRAL EASTERN POLAND

Prologue:

"Say hello to my future wife," Private Sam Wyatt declared to the rest of the room the moment the woman appeared on the television screen. The young soldier's eyes became bewitched with lust as he ogled the lithe figure of the journalist.

The announcement was met by a howl of good-natured jeers from the rest of the Americans in the barracks dayroom. Most of the off-duty men were arranged in a semi-circle of mismatched chairs in front of the TV screen. The cameraman filming the journalist zoomed in from a wide-shot to a close-up, and the mockery of Private Wyatt turned into a chorus of appreciative wolf-whistles for the beautiful woman on the television.

She was tall, her body perfectly proportioned. She was wearing tight-fitting denim jeans and a pink collared dress shirt, with the top two buttons undone to reveal just a hint of cleavage; enough to be noticed but not so much as to represent a blatant display of her sexuality.

"The fear in Warsaw is very real," the journalist moved across the screen as she talked. She was standing in the rubble of a bombed-out building in the Polish capital, her hands thrust deep into her pockets as she picked her way through the debris and delivered her report to camera. "Locals are living in fear; fear that once again, fighting and killing will tear Poland apart. With the Russian Army massed along the Lithuanian border, it seems the nightmares of the Second World War might soon return to western Europe."

Her dark hair hung down across her brow in a shimmering halo and cascaded over her shoulders, emphasizing her high Slavic cheekbones, the rounded softness of her face and the squareness of her jawline. Her hooded, sultry eyes were bright with intelligence, and the pout of her mouth as she spoke suggested determination and a spark of arrogant defiance. She reached the street corner and paused for a moment. In the background a firetruck's siren wailed as it rushed through a billowing grey column of smoke.

"Yesterday US military officials in Poland were saying that fighting in Warsaw seemed *inevitable*. Today those same high-ranking military experts are declaring that war is *imminent*." Her accent was unmistakably American, but her intonation of several key words as she continued to speak seemed faintly inflected.

The camera followed the journalist as she stepped past the façade of a burned-out restaurant, then stopped again. Behind her, on the opposite side of the street, stood a line of grim-faced Warsaw locals waiting by the doors of a NATO food and aid station.

"For almost eighty years these people and the peace-loving populations of Belarus, Poland and the Baltic States have lived under the dark menace of death and destruction," the journalist continued. "Today, it seems those nightmares are about to return as NATO commanders rush troops northeast towards the Suwalki Gap to provoke the Russian troops there. Only time will tell whether the fighting that seems certain to erupt will once again extend its shadow over Warsaw," she paused in her monologue for dramatic effect, "but if it does, the human toll from this latest tragic conflict will be devastating..."

Across the bottom of the screen a graphic appeared with a CMM News logo and the words, *"Janna Vidas reporting live from Warsaw."*

The journalist's somber summation of the impending battle for Poland cast a pall of gloom over the soldiers in the barracks dayroom.

"And while the NATO and Russian armies prepare for combat in the northeast of Poland, many influential American politicians back home are asking the question that no one in US military command or the US Government is willing to answer," the journalist paused before continuing. *"Why are American soldiers even fighting Europe's war, thousands of miles from home, when the war against the Chinese continues to rage across the Pacific?"*

"Wyatt!" a commanding voice suddenly barked from the doorway of the dayroom, startling the soldiers transfixed to the TV screen. "Turn that liberal anti-war horse-shit off, god-dammit!"

The man in the doorway had his fists clenched, his face an angry snarl. He gave the beautiful female journalist on the screen a long last contemptuous look of disdain before the monitor turned black and silence filled the room. The rest of the troops in the dayroom scrambled to their feet and stood stiffly at attention.

"There's no place in this man's Army for left-wing bleeding-heart opinions," Lieutenant Colonel Karl Armstrong cowered the assembled enlisted men with the steely force of his gaze. He was simmering with temper. "If you want to know what's going on in this war, then ask your officers – don't listen to some anti-war Democrat journalist. Am I clear?"

"Yes, sir!" the men in the room snapped.

Armstrong swept his gaze around the room, making eye contact with every single soldier before he spoke again. "We are the 173rd Sky Soldiers (Airborne Brigade) and you're all fighting men. This isn't the Air Force; we don't have the luxury of emotions or sentiment. Every one of you is a warrior and armed conflict is what we're training for. So start acting like soldiers, god-dammit, and stop listening to all the horse-shit our Liberal media is spreading."

Armstrong withered the soldiers with the scorn of his gaze for a few seconds more, and then turned on his heel and stormed out of the room; his boots sounding like pounding drums as he disappeared into the night.

The Colonel knew instinctively as he marched across the parade ground towards his office that he had made a mistake; the way to lead men was not through brow-beating and berating them. The way to lead was through building a bond and sharing hardships. He had let his temper get the better of him, and now Karl Armstrong regretted his tirade. But he knew too that action had been necessary. TV network news was a powerful influencer, and the last thing that fighting men needed on the eve of imminent war was a head full of doubts and confusion about the virtue of their mission.

He was still berating himself for acting like a jackass when he recognized a young adjutant waiting for him by the door of his office, holding a printout in his hand.

"What is it, Rizzo?"

"A message from US Headquarters in Warsaw, sir," the young junior officer offered the paperwork to his commanding officer.

Armstrong grunted and pushed open his office door, peeling off his jacket as he strode into the small room. He flicked on his desk lamp. "Just give me the guts of it."

"Yes, sir," the man cleared his throat. "HQ wants to inform you that two Platoons of Abrams tanks will be arriving here at the Biala Podlaska Training Base tomorrow for joint training exercises, as per a request from the Polish Government. Oh, and there will also be VIPs arriving from the capital. You're ordered to afford them every possible assistance while they're here."

"What?" Karl Armstrong turned and roared, spots of livid temper burning on his cheeks. He clawed his hands through his hair and gaped at the young officer, aghast. "What fucking request for Abrams tanks? I didn't ask for any god-damned tanks. We're training the Polish on field artillery and howitzer drills."

The adjutant shrugged, then winced. "It seems as though the Polish Government made the request, sir. Maybe through Major Nowak?"

"Jesus Christ!" Armstrong shook his head as a storm of anger washed over him. His mind latched on to the second piece of news, and he growled his temper again. "And who are these fucking VIPs? I haven't got time to be kissing the ass of Washington politicians right now. We're supposed to be in the middle of a god-damned war!"

"The message doesn't say, sir," Rizzo offered meekly. "It just insists that we afford the VIPs every possible assistance."

Lieutenant Colonel Karl Armstrong threw himself down into the chair behind his cluttered desk and closed his eyes, seething. His breathing came in a series of angry snorts, like a bull about to charge. The adjutant backed out of the room and closed the commanding officer's door quietly behind him.

*

Karl Armstrong sat for a long time in total silence; his emotions a torment of bitter frustration. He swore under his breath, his jaw clenched and his hands balled into fists. He was a career infantry officer who had first served as a Lieutenant Platoon leader in the 82nd Airborne with follow-on assignments as a Company Commander before staff time as a Major in a Battalion S-3 section. He had first gone into combat at the beginning of the Global War on Terror in Iraq and had been fighting ever since, most recently as a Company commander in Afghanistan with the 173rd Airborne Brigade.

Now, on the eve of the biggest conflict the world had seen in eight decades, he was commanding a Company of 173rd paratroopers and a Company of combat engineers on a training field in central eastern Poland, tutoring a Battalion of Polish troops on the fundamentals of fighting with artillery support while thousands of other American soldiers were on the frontlines and preparing for war against the Russians.

Karl Armstrong was a patriot. He had joined the military to serve his country. He believed he could do that more effectively with an M4 in his hands and an enemy in front of him than he could tied down to a desk at an isolated training base close to the Belarusian border.

The lamp cast a pale glow over the paperwork around him but left the corners of the office in deep shadow. Armstrong turned in his chair and looked out at the dark brooding night. He stared into space, his exasperation simmering to the boil. He wanted to get into the fight. He was an experienced combat officer; he should be leading men into action, not training raw recruits.

His eyes drifted back around the darkened room and settled on a black patch of wall where a framed guidon with a coin and a small brass plaque hung. The memento had been presented to him by the combat Company he had commanded in Wardak Province, Afghanistan, as part of Task Force Bayonet. Beside it, he knew, were framed Brigade citations awarded to him during more recent combined operation exercises into Latvia and Ukraine.

With an impulsive rush, he swept the folders of paperwork aside, and powered up his laptop computer. After a last moment of contemplation, he began to compose an email requesting an immediate transfer to a combat posting in northern Poland.

It was the third transfer request he had emailed to Command Headquarters in Vincenza, Italy, in the past ten days, and the bitterness poured out of him in a fury of resentment as his fingers dashed across the keyboard. He punched the 'send' button and then swarmed to his office door.

"Cranston!" he barked for his orderly.

A young staff officer appeared in the hallway, harassed and bleary-eyed. "Sir?"

"Cranston, I'm going fishing at dawn tomorrow morning. I need a couple of hours away from this place. Wake the XO up and tell him he's coming too. Tell him it's a direct order."

THE FRONTIER OF BELARUS
NORTHWEST OF BREST

Chapter 1:

Colonel Hvejdar Stanyuta, commanding the lead elements of the Belarusian Army's 11th Guards Mechanized Brigade, stood near the banks of the Bug River and stared west into the darkening sunset sky. Fifty-five years old, Stanyuta was a career soldier who had joined the Belarusian Army as a teenager and had quickly been identified as a future military leader. He had attended the Minsk Suvorov Military school, and then the Ul'yanovsk Guards Suvorov Military School, excelling and impressing his Russian tutors with his intuitive tactical understanding of ground force combat situations. From there his career was fast-tracked, and his rise through the ranks of the Belarusian military meteoric. After commanding a tank company in Southern Group, he had been sent to the famous Malinovsky Military Armored Forces Academy soon after it had merged with the Frunze Military Academy to become the Combined Arms Academy in 1998.

Now he was Deputy Commander of Western Operational Command, and the man who had been given the responsibility for launching a Belarusian Army invasion into central Poland that would ultimately link up with the Russian Armies about to pour across the Suwalki Gap further to the north.

But for all his career accomplishments to date – or maybe because of those experiences – Colonel Stanyuta was pensive and subdued as he stared across the river into eastern Poland.

Gathered around him stood a huddle of aides and junior officers, and there were more staff a few hundred yards away, clustered around Stanyuta's BTR-80AK command vehicle.

The Colonel took a last fretful look at the sky overhead. As nightfall had approached, so had storm clouds. Now the darkening skyline was thick with brooding menace, threatening a downpour at any moment. Stanyuta sighed. Not even the best laid plans could account for the weather…

"Has there been any sign – any sign at all – that the Polish are alerted to our presence?" he asked the question without turning. A Major from Army intelligence standing nearby answered.

"None, sir," the Major replied. "We've been monitoring the enemy's troop movements for the past ten days. They appear completely unaware of our Army's presence along the border."

Stanyuta grunted. "No signs of them fortifying their positions?"

"No, sir," the Major answered. "The Polish troops defending the border posts across from us remain minimal; a few APCs and a handful of light infantry dispersed between the two main crossing points. Their attention seems to be focused to the northeast where our Russian brothers are preparing to attack through the Suwalki Gap."

"You're quite sure of that?"

The Major hesitated, wary of being caught out in a blatant lie. "Well…" he blustered, "some of our intelligence sources are HUMINT; Polish civilians moving back and forth across the border. Their testimonies can never be relied upon completely. And several of our own spies are yet to report in with their most recent observations…"

"So, you're not certain?" Stanyuta wheeled on the Major. The Colonel was a fearsome-looking bull of a man, with a thick thatch of greying hair, steely eyes and a jagged scar that ran down his right cheek from the outside of his eye to the corner of his mouth.

"Our… our Air Force has been flying reconnaissance flights close to the border for the past five days. They have reported no movement on the far side of the river, and we have had nothing passed on to us from our Russian comrades operating their photoreconnaissance satellites, Colonel."

"Has there been any updates from ZOK (Western Operational Command) or the Ministry of Defense in Minsk?"

"Nothing in the past six hours, Colonel."

Again, Stanyuta grunted. The dubious quality of his intelligence was another misgiving to add to a long list of concerns he had about this looming operation.

"Are the bridging engineers ready?"

"Yes, comrade Colonel," a smartly-uniformed Captain of Engineers stepped forward. "I have supervised their dispositions personally."

Stanyuta eyed the Captain suspiciously. The young man stood stiffly at attention, his eyes bright with patriotic fervor. For this young fool, Stanyuta guessed, the prospect of war was something he eagerly anticipated.

"Are the engineers fully equipped?"

"Yes, Colonel," the Captain replied smartly.

"And have they been briefed? Are they certain of their mission?"

"I conducted the briefings personally, comrade Colonel."

Stanyuta nodded. "Very well." On the far side of the river, he could see the little pinpricks of house lights as nightfall arrived. "Have the bridging engineers notified. We cross the Bug River at 0300 hours. I want those ribbon bridges assembled and in readiness by 0200. And if they're not in place, Captain, I'll want your resignation. Understood?"

"Yes, comrade Colonel!" the young Captain snapped a salute.

Colonel Stanyuta turned from the riverbank and strode through the scrub towards his BTR-80AK, his head down and his thoughts brooding. His plan was a simple one; use ribbon bridges to put his scouting elements across the river to first secure the Polish crossing points and several key roads, and then pour his troops and tanks over the bridge at Brest into central Poland. Once the Polish border region had been overwhelmed, he would drive west under the umbrella of massed mobile artillery, his forces sweeping aside NATO resistance as they bulldozed remorselessly west towards Warsaw.

He would have preferred the promise of more air support, but his real concern was the quality of the troops Western

Operational Command had given him for the mission, and the condition of their equipment.

The soldiers were B-rate recruits – many of them conscripts and inexperienced troopers who were newly arrived to the border from training barracks around Minsk. Only a few of his officers had any Russian military training, and his tanks were poorly maintained due to several years of Government budget cuts that had stripped the nation's military bare. All Stanyuta had in his favor was the element of surprise and an overwhelming advantage in numbers. According to old Soviet doctrine those two elements would be sufficient to ensure victory.

When the Colonel reached his command vehicle, he singled out his supply officer and drew him away from the clutch of staff members. "Major Ignatik, bring me up to date with the supply situation."

Once his tanks, APCs and troops were into central Poland, Stanyuta would need a steady flow of diesel to keep his armor and all the infantry transport trucks in the column moving – and he couldn't count on seizing NATO fuel dumps intact along the way.

"Everything is in order, Colonel," Major Ignatik saluted. The man had the features of a harried, overworked public servant. "You will have all the diesel you need to reach Warsaw, comrade Colonel. My life on it."

"Yes," Stanyuta said bluntly. "That is what is at stake, Major. Your life, and the lives of all the troops we send into battle, so you had better not fail me."

The Major disappeared back into the throng of aides and Colonel Stanyuta paused to light a cigarette. Now the decision to attack had been made and he was committed to battle, he felt a soldier's fatalism. He had done all he could to maintain the element of surprise and he had a straight-forward plan that neither relied on finesse or timing. The attack would be a battering ram; a tidal wave of metal and men in the old Soviet manner.

It would work.

It had to work.

*

The Belarusian Army bridging engineers steered their 6x6 off-road KrAZ-255 trucks up to the east bank of the Bug River carrying folded sections of ribbon bridge atop their vehicles. It was 0100 hours, and under the watchful eye of the Engineers Captain, the first bridging section splashed into the water, unfolding open to form the initial span of road across the river.

Waiting patiently in a wooded clump of beech and pine trees that fringed the Bug were a handful of Belarusian Army BRDM-2 Amphibious Armored Scout cars. The Senior Lieutenant commanding the assault stood chain-smoking cigarettes as he watched the engineers at work. His two Platoons of vehicles would be the first troops into enemy territory.

The location was a wooded stretch of terrain three kilometers north of the Terespol-Brest border crossing point, but there were other scouting units making similar raids to the south of his position and to the north, closer to the Kukuryki-Kozlowiczy border crossing point. All in all, some thirty Belarusian Army BRDM-2s and their crews would comprise the pointed tip of the invading army's spear, crossing into Poland from four separate locations.

The mission for the scouting units was critical; they were to secure the key bridgeheads across the Bug River at Terespol and Kukuryki, and then push further west, sweeping aside isolated pockets of Polish resistance before the main force swarmed into Poland at dawn.

By 0215 hours the bridge across the river was assembled and the engineers threw down their tools, exhausted and soaking wet. The Senior Lieutenant commanding the scouting force glanced at his wristwatch. There was still forty-five minutes before he could launch his attack across the river;

three-quarters of an hour in which a curious Polish border patrol might stumble upon the bridge and raise the alarm.

The Senior Lieutenant walked down the column of scout cars under his command, talking quietly to each man. The drivers and radio operators – and the handful of infantry that would be hitching an uncomfortable ride on the rear deck of each vehicle – were sitting in the grass nervously smoking cigarettes and drinking vodka-laced coffee. Only each vehicle's gunner, hunched behind the trigger of the 14.5mm KPVT heavy machine gun in the small conical turret of each scout car, remained aboard and on watch. The commanders of each BRDM-2 were huddled in a small group between two of the scout cars, poring over maps with last-minute anxiety.

"We're going early," the Senior Lieutenant announced as he approached the knot of men. It was a relief to some and a dreadful shock to others. The faces of the vehicle commanders that stared back at the Senior Lieutenant were pale and questioning in the darkness. "There's no point sitting around with our cocks in our hands, waiting to see if the Polish discover the bridges before we can attack. So, we're crossing early," he explained his decision and then checked his wristwatch again. "Get your men organized and get the infantry mounted up. I want to be on the far bank and ready to move on the bridgehead in twenty minutes."

*

The Belarusian BRDM-2s crossed the ribbon bridge in low gear and disappeared into the darkness on the far bank of the Bug River. Once on enemy soil, the Senior Lieutenant ordered the vehicles to speed south towards Terespol.

Following the serpentine undulations of the riverbank, the six vehicles raced across country. A dirt trail appeared between clumps of forest and the scout cars accelerated. The track through the woods led southeast, directly to the Terespol-Brest border crossing facility, five hundred yards west of the bridge. Even in the middle of the night the complex was lit by towering arc lights that illuminated two vast carports and a myriad of buildings between parking lots. Signposted across the awning of one covered shelter were the words, *Przejscie Graniczne Terespol.*

The six Belarusian BRDM-2s caught the Platoon of Polish border guards by complete surprise. Bursting from the tree line with their 7.62mm turret-mounted coaxial machine guns blazing, they charged into the floodlit arena. Once inside the perimeter of the checkpoint, the infantry mounted on the back of each scout car leaped to the ground and ran for the nearest buildings.

Half the Polish infantry on late-night duty were standing idly by the entry gates that blocked the road to the bridge. They were cut down in the first few furious seconds of the attack. The rest of the soldiers were asleep in a barracks building on the perimeter of the complex. The Belarusian soldiers threw grenades through the ground-floor windows and as the explosions rocked the interior, they charged through the front doors, firing through the smoke and sudden carnage, killing everyone inside.

A single Polish BMP-1 AIFV was stationed at the Terespol crossing point. The vehicle was a relic of Soviet design; an amphibious armored infantry fighting vehicle that had first appeared in the 1960s. The unmanned BMP-1 was parked broadside beneath one of the massive awnings, lit by banks of fluorescent lighting. A Belarusian infantryman fired an RPG-7 at the vehicle. The operator disappeared behind a puff of light blue smoke as the projectile streaked towards its target.

The Polish AIFV was consumed in a sheet of flames and a thunderclap of noise. The projectile smashed into the thin side armor and tore the vehicle apart. The shattered hulk erupted in a tower of oily black smoke.

The battle for the bridgehead was over in just a few furious minutes. In the smoking, stinking aftermath of the firefight, the Belarusian infantry wandered amongst the Polish dead, scavenging watches, jewelry and rifling pockets for money, turning each bloodied corpse over to frisk the remains. Shots rang out across the dark night as two wounded enemy soldiers were quickly dispatched. The Belarusian troops chattered volubly amongst themselves as they completed their gruesome work, relieved at the ease in which they had won victory. One of the soldiers found a hip-flask filled with alcohol on a dead Polish trooper and drank greedily. More bottles of spirits were discovered when the locked door to a storage building was smashed down.

The Senior Lieutenant surveyed the battleground with grim satisfaction and a sigh of relief. It had been a well-executed surprise attack. He ordered his radio operator to contact command headquarters. "Tell them the Terespol crossing point has been secured and that the bridge is open. Tell them we are moving west." As he spoke, he groped for a map and held it up to the light. "There is a small settlement two kilometers to the west called Branztyin. Tell command that is where we are headed."

*

Alicija Symanski woke with a jolt of formless foreboding and rolled her head on the pillow to check the baby's cot, then the time. It was three o'clock in the morning. The baby slept soundly, but Alicija's sense of unease persisted. Beside her, her husband snored, his unshaven face covered beneath a crumple of blankets. She rose naked from the bed, wrapped herself in a dressing gown, and moved to the window. For a moment the night around the hamlet of Branztyin remained pitch black, and then she heard the rumble of heavy engines. Suddenly shadows moved across the settlement's single narrow street and a split-second later she heard the sound of a window smashing, followed by a burst of flickering flame from within a nearby home.

Quietly, but with an urgent edge to her voice, she called to her husband.

"Jakub!"

A terrified shout from somewhere in the night startled her and she called out to her husband again, this time more urgently.

"Jakub! Wake up!"

The distant shout became a scream of agonized pain, cut short by the unmistakable whip-crack of a rifle shot. The wicked retort seemed to echo on the air. Alicija reached for the baby and when she returned to the window, the child cradled in her arms, the street was lit by leaping flames and there were silhouettes of armed running men, moving across the lurid light. Another shot rang out, then a stutter of automatic fire. Another agonized cry of terror split the night. A handful of the dark figures ran past Alicija's bedroom window… and then the sounds of their pounding footsteps stopped abruptly. Alicija felt her heart leap into her throat.

When the front door burst inwards under the heel of a swinging boot, Alicija screamed. The baby in her arms came awake howling. She turned to face the bedroom door, her eyes wide with terror. She could hear stampeding feet and furniture being overturned. Glass smashed and then she heard the gruff, drunken voices of many men. Her husband came awake a moment before the bedroom door burst open and three Belarusian soldiers stood framed in the threshold.

"What the –?" Alicija's husband sat bolt upright. One of the soldiers shot the man between the eyes, then turned his leering lecherous gaze on the young blonde woman by the window.

Alicija screamed in shock and then rising wide-eyed terror.

The three Belarusian soldiers swarmed across the room. One of them tore the infant from Alicija's arms and hurled the crying baby out through the window. The two remaining soldiers dragged the young woman kicking and screaming to the bed, tearing the robe from her shoulders as they pinned her to the mattress.

The night was bright with flames as the first of the Belarusian scout cars trundled into view. The lead BRDM-2 braked to a halt at the nearest intersection and the vehicle's turret turned a slow circle, the 14.5mm KPVT heavy machine gun spitting flame and death as its roaring gun hosed every building in the Polish settlement with a hail of hammering gunfire.

When the machine gun fell silent, the rest of the waiting Belarusian infantry swarmed forward, entering each house in turn. Men and children were pushed out into the night and executed on the sidewalk. The cowering women were dragged into the street and pack-raped. Then the Belarusian soldiers ransacked the hamlet, looting each house for alcohol until the leaping flames drove them back into the night. They prowled the narrow road, drunk and baying like wild animals, stopping intermittently to take their turn on one of the naked women or to fire wildly into the bullet-riddled corpses that lay slumped in the gutter.

The Senior Lieutenant snapped at his radio-operator to contact command. "Tell them Branztyin is secure," he gruffed. "And tell them we are awaiting further orders."

The reply from command was almost immediate. The vehicle's radio crackled to life, the connection hissing with static. The radio operator listened intently, asked for the message to be repeated, and then acknowledged.

"We are to push on towards the crossroads at Wolka Dobrynska, comrade commander," the operator relayed the order.

"Where the fuck is that?" the Senior Lieutenant reached again for the map in his pocket.

"It's about ten kilometers west," the radio operator explained. "That is where the roads from the bridges at Brest and Kukuryki converge. Command wants the intersection secured by dawn."

The Senior Lieutenant grunted. He dismounted his vehicle through the commander's hatch and stood in the middle of the street, his hands on his hips. Three soldiers appeared from the doorway of a nearby house dragging a young naked blonde woman with them. She hung limp in their arms, her head lolling, her tender body bruised and beaten.

"Is the bitch dead?" the Senior Lieutenant snapped with sudden interest.

The three soldiers looked momentarily struck with guilt and alarm. "No, sir," one of the men answered.

"Good," the officer reached for the fastening of his belt. "Dump her on the grass over there. I want one of you men to stay behind to hold her down. The other two can return to your vehicles. We move out in fifteen minutes."

*

The early reports coming in sporadically from across the Bug were promising, Colonel Stanyuta admitted grudgingly. All of his scouting parties had crossed into the frontier of Poland undetected, and the first pre-dawn attacks on Polish outposts had been completed successfully. The bridgeheads at Brest and Kukuryki were secure, and now all that mattered was reaching a key crossroads ten kilometers west of the border, at a village named Wolka Dobrynska. Once the crossroads were seized and the village secure, he could pour his troops and tanks across the Bug *en masse*.

He stubbed out a cigarette and strode towards his command vehicle with its two tall whip antennae at each of the rear corners and leaned in through the open hatch to hear the latest report from his operations officer.

The interior of the BTR-80AK was packed with radio communication equipment and a small team of operators, working shoulder-to-shoulder in the cramped confines.

"I need a briefing," the Colonel demanded.

The operations officer bobbed his head obediently and reached for a wad of scribbled notes. "We are a little behind schedule," the officer delivered the bad news first. "All our scouting units crossed the Bug successfully and have secured the nearest border settlements. So far, we have reports of just two men killed, with no damage to any vehicles. Polish resistance was lighter than we anticipated, although the few troops they had posted at the Kukuryki crossing point fought valiantly for almost fifteen minutes before they were overcome."

Stanyuta grunted. "How far behind schedule are we?"

"Thirty minutes, comrade Colonel. Our lead elements that secured the Brest bridgehead should have been at Wolka Dobrynska by now… but they are still some distance away."

"Are there any indications that Polish Command in Warsaw is aware of our attack or is mobilizing to confront us?"

The operations officer hesitated and his face flushed with sudden color. "We have had no word of any Polish troop movements in the past few hours… but communications with Minsk are intermittent."

"So, for all we know, the entire Polish Army and their NATO allies could be massing and moving to intercept us?"

"It's very unlikely, comrade Colonel…"

"But it's fucking possible!" Stanyuta slammed his clenched fist against the steel frame of the hatch. "Because our intelligence network is as piss-poor as the troops and vehicles I have been given to fight this fucking war!" his voice rose, seething with bitter contempt.

"Why don't I know the strength of the enemy in front of me? Because our intelligence is second-rate and dependent on the morsels fed to us by our Russian brothers in Moscow," he began counting off his criticisms on his fingers as his temper broke into a rage. "And why are we already behind schedule? Because our vehicles are poorly maintained, and rarely serviced due to budget cuts!" he seethed. "And as for the men? Christ! They're untrained raw recruits from the depots in Minsk with barely enough experienced junior officers to lead them."

The Colonel spun away and stared into the brooding night sky. He longed to be in his T-72 and charging into battle, with an enemy in front of him and the warrior's red mist in his eyes – not standing impotently on the side of the highway outside Brest while a column of unreliable vehicles and B-rate troops awaited his orders.

Within the command vehicle a radio suddenly sparked to life and through a hiss of static Stanyuta heard one of his scouting elements in Poland make their report. He turned, his temper still simmering, and waited for the update.

"Our lead elements are approaching Wolka Dobrynska as we speak," the operations officer's voice betrayed his relief.

Stanyuta checked his wristwatch. "They should have been there forty minutes ago," he growled. "Tell them they need to move faster. I want that crossroads secured before 0400 hours."

He was just about to turn away when his intelligence officer appeared out of the night. The man's face was dark with foreboding. He caught the Colonel's eye and held up a folded piece of paper. "For you, comrade Colonel. A disturbing report I think you should see."

Stanyuta snatched the folded page and read it quickly. As his eyes scanned the paper his facial features changed, tightening with temper until he was shaking with anger. He glared at the intelligence officer. "Is this true?" he waved the page.

"I believe it is," the other man nodded grimly.

"God-damn it to hell!" Stanyuta raged. He hauled his operations officer physically from the interior of the BTR-80AK, seizing the man by the scruff of his collar.

"Read this!" he thrust the page in the shaken officer's pale face.

Reports were filtering in from Poland that the small settlement of Branztyin had been razed to the ground, every man and child murdered, and every woman raped. The buildings had been looted and the Belarusian troops who had executed the raid were allegedly drunk.

For several years discipline within the Belarusian Army had been deteriorating. Reports of indiscipline, corruption and alcoholism were rife; conditions attributed to the poor state of the nation's armed forces and the Army's inability to retain officers. Between 2011 and 2015, almost half of the young officers left military service before completing their contract period – and of the more than five hundred graduates at officer training schools in the previous year, only ten percent were still in the nation's military or security forces. They were grim signs of a military in decay. For decades the Belarusian Army had been heavily reliant on Soviet and Russian training and had been run with a Russian-styled structure. Now the failings of recent years were having real-world consequences. Not only were the men under the Colonel's command little more than a thug-like undisciplined rabble, but barely half of them were properly equipped or wearing body armor.

"I… I don't know what to say…" the operations officer's face drained of color.

"I fucking do!" Stanyuta roared. It didn't bother him that the Polish citizens of a stinking little hovel had been murdered and raped. He could care less. It bothered him that his troops were drunk and looting when a vital crossroads needed to be seized. "Tell the Senior Lieutenant in command of that unit to capture Wolka Dobrynska immediately. Once the village and roads are under our control, I want that bastard brought to me – dead or alive. Understand?"

The operations officer nodded quickly, withered by the force of the Colonel's towering rage. "I will give the orders personally, comrade Colonel."

*

At 0415 hours three Belarusian scouting Platoons launched a coordinated attack to seize the crossroads at Wolka Dobrynska, closing on the tiny settlement from the north, south and east simultaneously. The dismounted infantry led the assault, storming forward and firing indiscriminately into the cluster of community buildings. They rampaged through the village like a wild horde of marauding raiders, plundering and killing until they were slaked with blood.

A Platoon of Polish light infantry billeted in the village were caught unprepared and overwhelmed. The Polish Lieutenant was captured in the brief firefight and was dragged into the main street. A crowd of Belarusian troops surrounded the young officer and kicked him to death.

The BRDM-2s took up hull-down positions in the burning ruins, covering the road west to Warsaw.

On the verge of the road outside Brest, Colonel Stanyuta received the report the crossroads had been seized with a sigh of relief. He checked his watch. The attack was slipping further behind schedule.

"Radio the tanks in the lead Battalion with a flash order to get moving across the bridge!" the Colonel barked at his operations officer. "And be ready to follow them west. I want to be at that crossroads in Poland in one hour to take direct command of the situation."

*

The vanguard of the Belarusian invasion force comprised three Battalions of T-72 tanks. The vehicles were assembled along the verge of the highway at Brest, awaiting instructions. Once the flash order reached the lead tank, they moved quickly, rumbling past the Colonel's command vehicle in a heroic procession as they dashed across the Polish frontier.

Twenty minutes after the last Battalion tank had disappeared into the western night, Colonel Stanyuta climbed aboard his command vehicle and followed the armor into enemy territory.

When he arrived on the outskirts of the Polish settlement at Wolka Dobrynska, very little of the village remained undamaged. Most of the building and homes around the crossroads had been burned to the ground, and there were bodies of civilians and Polish soldiers lying in the streets. More dead had been dragged to the corner and piled into a bloody mound. The corpses were bloated, turning purple and crawling with flies. The stench of death was thick in the still air.

Colonel Stanyuta dismounted his command vehicle and ran a critical eye across the site, noting the defensive positions of the BRDM-2s. He strode forward, beyond the outskirts of the village and stood for a moment in the silent night, his senses alert. He could hear no enemy aircraft in the sky, nor sense the rumble of approaching enemy armor. He grunted, satisfied, and returned to the village taking long purposeful strides. His eyes were everywhere, noting everything. He saw two T-72s parked on the shoulder of the road, the vehicles abandoned.

"What happened here?" he demanded of the nearest officer. "I thought the settlement had been secured by our scouts. How were these two tanks knocked out?"

"They weren't, comrade Colonel," the tank officer sounded apologetic and embarrassed. "Both tanks broke down with mechanical problems. We can't repair them until we receive the necessary spare parts, but they are in the supply vehicles at the rear of the column."

"Christ!" the Colonel swore bitterly. "Our scouting units will be fanning out and pushing west at sunrise, and I need these MBTs right behind them," Stanyuta stabbed his finger at the tank officer. "Make sure both vehicles are fully operational before dawn."

The Colonel stormed off into the night, simmering and also troubled. His poorly-maintained T-72s were already breaking down, and they were barely ten kilometers into enemy territory…

Chapter 2:

Standing knee deep in the frigid waters of the reservoir with the stub of a cigar wedged into the corner of his mouth and a baseball cap pulled down low over his eyes, Karl Armstrong carefully whipped the lightweight fishing rod back over his shoulder and then cast towards a bank of reeds thirty feet from where he stood. The thin line spooled off the reel, and the float sailed across the still water and landed with a soft splash just a few feet from his target. Armstrong grunted, satisfied, and turned a wary soldier's eye towards the sky.

It was still an hour before sunrise but already the horizon was lit with a pre-dawn glow of watery light, filtering through the trees. The reservoir was located fifteen kilometers southwest of the Biala Podlaska training camp; a tranquil grove of grassland and woods around a trout fishing paradise.

Standing on the bank in long grass, Armstrong's Executive Officer, Major Charles Mott, made a grunt of grudging approval. "Not bad," he conceded to acknowledge Armstrong's cast. "Reckon you'll miss all this when you transfer?"

Karl Armstrong turned his head and scowled. "What the hell are you talking about, Charlie?"

Mott shrugged and finished fiddling with his rig. "The word around the base is that you sent off another request to Headquarters for a transfer to a fighting unit last night…"

"Aw, Christ!" Armstrong growled. "How did you hear about that?"

Again, Mott shrugged. "It's a small base. Is it true?"

"Yeah."

For a long moment there was silence between the two men. Finally, Mott nodded. "Karl, I'm starting to think you don't like my company…"

Armstrong snatched the cigar from the corner of his mouth and came wading from the water. There was a thermos flask of coffee in the grass beside his fishing gear. He dropped down to the ground, his expression suddenly serious.

"Charlie, we're soldiers. We've fought in the same mud and spilled the same blood. We don't belong here in the ass-end of nowhere filling in time like a couple of semi-retired school teachers. We're combat soldiers. We belong on the front lines where we can make a real difference to the outcome of this war. This isn't like any previous mission – this is the real deal against the Russians. And I don't want to miss it."

"You're making a difference here, right now, to those Polish recruits we're training," the XO pointed out reasonably.

"Yeah. Maybe. And in twelve months' time, if they continue to receive good training from experienced instructors, they will be fine fighting men," Karl Armstrong conceded. "But, Charlie, the war is about to happen any day now – not in twelve months. And once the Ruskies come across the Suwalki Gap, our boys are going to need experienced leaders. Dammit – it's the whole reason I joined the Army. I wanted to fight to defend my nation's freedom. Well, this is that fight!"

"Have you had a response from Headquarters?"

"No."

Mott nodded. He sat for a long moment staring out across the tranquil water of the reservoir alone with his thoughts. He understood Karl Armstrong's desire to join the frontlines. The two men had been a command team for almost a decade, fighting together across the Middle East and into Afghanistan. They knew each other intuitively; could read each other's thoughts and moods. It was the bond of shared fears and triumphs that had made them such an effective leadership team.

"When do you expect a reply?"

Armstrong grunted. "When hell freezes over," he muttered darkly and his frustration came simmering to the surface again. "Or when the fighting is finished and the war is over."

The Polish Army Ford Ranger 4WD the two men had driven to the reservoir was parked two hundred yards back along a dirt trail, screened by a dense grove of birch trees. Armstrong poured himself a cup of coffee, drank quickly, and then pushed himself to his feet. For a moment he thought he smelled diesel exhaust, but dismissed the notion almost as quickly as the idea registered. "I asked young Cranston to organize sandwiches for us. They're on the back seat of the 4WD. You hungry?"

Armstrong stepped out of his waterproof fishing waders and struck out for the Ford Ranger. Part way along the dirt trail he stopped suddenly, like a hunting dog, his senses instantly alert.

He turned back to the reservoir and saw the same frown of alarm on Charlie Mott's face. The two men locked eyes and Armstrong wordlessly pointed through the trees to the west of where they stood.

Armstrong ducked low and went into the fringe of the woods at a crouch. Mott ghosted to his shoulder; the two soldiers suddenly tensed and on edge. Somewhere beyond where they were hidden, and through a veil of trees, both men could hear a diesel engine and the sound of undergrowth being pushed aside by heavy tires.

Wordlessly the two veteran American paratroopers crawled forward through the thick undergrowth until the trees around them thinned and suddenly they were laying in the long grass staring at three BRDM-2 armored cars. The vehicles were painted forest green and sprayed with white camouflage patterns, the boat-shaped hulls slathered in spattered mud and grime. The BRDMs were parked in a small clearing, surrounded by high trees and thick foliage with their engines running. Moving around the idle vehicles were small groups of armed soldiers. The men were wearing camouflage gear and body armor, their faces streaked with painted lines to conceal their skin. Each soldier carried an AK-74 assault rifle, and on their shoulders they wore a badge bearing the Belarusian flag.

Karl Armstrong gaped in astonished shock for a long moment, his mind racing and his heart quickening. He turned his head towards Mott, and his expression was incredulous.

The Belarusian Army has crossed the border into Poland!

Mott was just as aghast as his Lieutenant Colonel. The two men lay very still and watched the enemy soldiers. The

Belarusian scouts had stopped to relieve themselves in the grass and to heat up bland Russian-issued IRP ration packs (*individual'nyi Ratsion Pitaniya*). The enemy soldiers were casual and relaxed, chatting easily amongst themselves as the odor of kerosene from the small burners wafted on the air. They dropped down into the long grass close to the BRDM-2s. Some men stretched out and closed their eyes. Others sat cleaning their weapons and smoking. A bottle of vodka was passed around and the infantry drank greedily. Finally, an officer appeared from behind the hull of the far armored car. He was a dark-haired narrow-shouldered man with a face covered in dust and grime. His uniform jacket was unbuttoned to the waist, and he had a sweaty neckerchief tied at his throat. He intercepted the bottle of spirits being handed around the group and drank thirstily.

Karl Armstrong began to slither backwards on his stomach, moving with exaggerated care, holding his breath and keeping his eyes fixed on the enemy soldiers for any sign his hideaway had been detected. Charlie Mott waited until his Colonel had cleared the area unobserved before he made his own retreat.

On the far side of the palisade of trees the two Americans leaned close together, talking in strained urgent whispers.

"Fucking Belarusian scouts!" Karl Armstrong was still in a state of incredulous shock.

"How did they get across the border?"

"Christ knows!" Armstrong breathed. "But they're armed combat soldiers, Charlie. No one puts on a condom unless they're ready to fuck, and no one sends armed recon units across a border unless they're ready for a fight."

"Could this be an attack to secure the bridges across the Bug River… or maybe even an all-out invasion?"

Armstrong nodded grimly. "I think so…"

For several days NATOs intelligence focus had been on the vast Russian Armies massing along the Lithuania-Poland border, the Allies trying to anticipate the moment when the enemy's armored echelons would plough through the Suwalki Gap.

Had the Russians outfoxed NATO intelligence?

A Belarusian Army driving west from the border could cover the one-hundred-mile distance to the Polish capital in less than a single day of hard fighting, and if the Russian and Belarusian spearheads linked up, tens of thousands of NATO troops could be caught between the jaws of a steel pincer and annihilated.

"I reckon we've been blindsided, Charlie," Karl Armstrong's face worked with worry and agitation. "I think NATO's been made to look the wrong way and now our troops in Poland are going to get hit by a Belarusian left hook we never saw coming."

"We've got to get out of here," Charlie Mott's thoughts raced ahead. "We need to get back to base and raise the alarm. And we need to know what's happening at the border and exactly what we're up against. Then someone needs to figure out what units the Allies can cobble together to slow the Belarusian attack."

*

The two Americans moved stealthily, first skirting the reed banks of the reservoir, and then following the overgrown dirt path that led them towards the parked Ford 4WD. Part way along the uneven trail a sudden shouted voice from behind made both men freeze.

The voice was loud, the language Belarusian, and the tone a strident command. Neither Armstrong or Mott had any idea what was being said. Armstrong turned and glanced over his shoulder. He saw a Belarusian soldier standing amongst the same grove of trees the Americans had just slithered from, the man's silhouette dappled in deep shadow. He was clutching his unfastened pants to his waist with one hand and balancing an AK-74 clumsily in the other. His face was unshaven, his eyes wide. There was a hundred yards of open grassland between the Americans and the enemy soldier, and a hundred yards of dirt trail between the Americans and the parked 4WD.

"Are we going to take him on?" Charlie Mott spoke quietly from the corner of his mouth. In seconds the banks of the reservoir would be crawling with enemy troops, alerted by the soldier's cry of alarm.

Karl Armstrong nodded his head, and swallowed hard. The tension was a solid lump in his throat. "Let's go for it!"

The two men broke into a sudden sprint, their arms pumping as they dashed for the safety of the 4WD.

Charlie Mott ran for his life, lifting his legs high through the long grass as the rutted dirt path dipped beneath his pounding feet. He had the sensation of running in place; the sense that the Ford was coming no closer. He felt a trickle of chill sweat between his shoulder blades. Beside him, Karl Armstrong ran like a charging bull, his big muscled frame working hard to maintain a place at Mott's shoulder. His legs felt leaden as he jinked from side to side to throw off the enemy soldier's aim. The heavy tense silence hung over them both like an ominous threat.

The two paratroopers reached the end of the trail and put themselves to a sharp steep rise of grassy slope. At the top of the incline waited the Ford Ranger. The vehicle was parked overlooking the reservoir on a plateau of mud-baked earth.

"Keep going!" Armstrong clawed at the long tufts of stringy weeds with his hands to haul himself up the rise. His driving legs and heaving chest felt like they were on fire.

The sound of a rifle cracked suddenly; a wicked thunderclap of noise that ripped the tense silence apart and sent flocks of birds scattering from the treetops. The bullet slashed through the air about Charlie Mott's face, missing him by inches.

The two men reached the top of the incline just as a new flurry of enemy semi-automatic fire stitched the dirt at their feet. Armstrong crested the rise first and thrust his hand into his pocket for the car keys. The doors were unlocked. He flung open the driver's side door and dived headlong across the seat for cover just as the air around the vehicle was shredded by the cracking sound of a thousand hammering thunderclaps.

The windshield of the Ford exploded inwards, spraying Karl Armstrong with shattered glass. He heard more bullets strike the front left fender. Then Mott's swollen red face appeared at the passenger side of the vehicle. He wrenched the door open and scrambled into cover just as Armstrong fumbled the keys into the ignition and the Polish Army 4WD's engine roared into life.

The Ranger was one of almost six hundred the Polish Army had bought from Ford before the outbreak of war. It had modified sixteen-inch steel rims with run flat inserts and heavy-duty tires.

Armstrong threw the vehicle into reverse, wrenching the steering wheel hard to turn the Ford around and face it west. Through the shattered windshield he saw a handful of Belarusian scouts lining the edge of the woods. The enemy soldiers were kneeling and laying prone in the long grass, the muzzle flash of their weapons lighting the pre-sunrise gloom with a winking firelight.

There were no weapons in the 4WD. The two Americans were utterly defenseless. More enemy bullets clanged against the vehicle's bodywork and punched holes in the rear doors as the Ford's tires churned for purchase and then flung the vehicle forward in a wild spray of gravel.

"Get your head down!" Armstrong roared as he wrenched the wheel, his own frame scrunched down deep into the upholstery of the seat. The wind through the shattered windscreen was like a blast of ice, the air thick with dust as the vehicle careened off the trail and went roaring west through long grass.

The land around the reservoir was a patchwork of disused farm fields, littered with stretches of hedgerow, wire fencing and sprinkled with knots of wind-stunted trees. The 4WD hit a pothole and jounced hard. The sudden crunching impact sent a spine-jarring shudder through the Ford's chassis and threw the two men together savagely. More bullets flew in a hail of hot lead past the fleeing vehicle and then abruptly the morning fell eerily silent.

"We're out of sight," Charlie Mott stole a glance back through the rear window.

"That won't last for long," Karl Armstrong put the Ford to a wire fence and crashed through, his foot jammed down hard on the gas pedal. "Any minute now those three fucking scout cars are going to come after us."

"Reckon we can outrun them?"

"Well, we're dead if we can't…"

Armstrong steered left, cutting across an overgrown field until he picked up the dirt trail again that would take them northwest to the Polish training base at Biala Podlaska. The nose of the Ford tilted as the 4WD began to climb a gradual rise. On the skyline ahead of them, the day was breaking in a riot of gold and crimson, silhouetting the rooftops of several two-story buildings in the distance.

A deep-throated thunder of gunfire shattered the sunrise, sounding close overhead. Charlie Mott wrenched violently round in his seat. One of the Belarusian BRDM-2s had emerged from the woods by the reservoir and opened fire with its 14.5mm KPVT heavy machine gun. The range was long and the enemy armored car seemed unwilling to close the distance. It fired three times in short hammering bursts and long fingers of tracer streaked out across the dawn sky.

Karl Armstrong grunted with the effort as he slewed the Ford Ranger from side to side, kicking up a rooster-tail of rising dirt to camouflage their escape. Then finally they were at the crest of the rise and swooping down the other side, into cover and out of the enemy's sight.

Armstrong threw himself back into the driver's seat, the danger momentarily relieved. The Ford reached the cluster of buildings and Armstrong braked to a stop in the main street.

Ortel Ksiazecy Pierwszy was a humble little village with a population of just over a hundred souls. Most of them were gathered on the sidewalks, roused from their beds by the early morning hammer of machine gun fire. Their faces were tight with fretful fear as they peered east towards the rising sun.

There were clouds of black smoke on the skyline, being smeared across the horizon by a nagging breeze.

Armstrong clambered down from the Ford and paused for a moment to study the bullet-ravaged carcass of the 4WD. There was glass on the front seats and dashboard, and over a dozen bullet holes in the bodywork. The front left fender was stoved in and the tires were gummed thick with clumps of mud and grass.

He searched the faces of the nearest villagers, looking for signs of recognition in their eyes as he spoke. "I'm an American soldier. I'm an American soldier," he repeated urgently. "Does anyone speak English?"

An old man wearing a threadbare jacket shuffled forward from out of the milling bystanders. He had a face deeply creased by hardship and age; his eyes rheumy as he stared up at Armstrong. "I speak English," he said.

Armstrong seized the frail old man by the shoulders and pushed his face close, his voice loud and urgent. "Tell everyone they must evacuate the village," the American paratrooper insisted. "The Belarusian Army has crossed the border. They are in the woods down by the fishing reservoir. Do you understand?"

The old man nodded, alarm changing his features as the enormity of what he was being told suddenly struck him. He turned to the villagers and spoke in a rapid staccato of Polish.

"Tell them they must make their way to the Biala Podlaska army base," Karl Armstrong said. "There are Polish and more American soldiers like me there. We will help them all evacuate to safety, but they must get to the base quickly, before the Belarusian soldiers arrive and launch an attack."

Charlie Mott climbed down from the 4WD as Armstrong spoke to the old man. Mott went striding along the road east until he was standing on the outskirts of the settlement. He stared at the brooding sky and the rising columns of smoke thoughtfully, then cocked his ear and listened hard. He thought he could hear the rumble of heavy vehicles far away on the fitful breeze. The sound lasted for only a moment, but it was enough to fill the paratrooper Major with a sense of ominous foreboding.

When he returned to the vehicle, his face was dark with worry. "Karl, we gotta go," he seized Armstrong's arm. "I think the Belarusians are already across the Bug and they're heading this way," he turned and pointed at the smoke-scarred sky. "I can hear armor on the move. It's still in the distance, but that won't last for long. We've got to get back to the base and raise the alarm, right now!"

*

"Incompetent *svolacy!*" Colonel Stanyuta punched the map-table before him and swore bitterly. "Repeat the message! Tell me everything again."

The young radio operator who had taken the call in the rear compartment of the BTR-80AK swallowed nervously. The vehicle hit a pothole and everything not held down inside the speeding eight-wheeler was thrown to the ground.

"The radio report was from Scout Platoon Five-One, comrade Colonel," the operator licked dry lips. "The commander radioed to report a contact with two Polish civilians in a 4WD."

"Where, exactly?"

The operator gave the grid coordinates. The Colonel snatched up a map of the Polish frontier from the floor of the armored personnel carrier and traced the location with his fingertip. It was a site southwest of a small Polish village named Piszczac, five kilometers south of the main highway that would ultimately carry his Mechanized Brigade all the way to the gates of Warsaw.

The Colonel grunted. "Why did the two civilians escape?"

The operator shrugged. "The report only said that two men were sighted near a reservoir. They were fired upon but evaded capture. They were last seen in a 4WD driving towards a village named Ortel Ksiazecy Pierwszy." The young operator mangled the pronunciation so badly that it took the

Colonel two full minutes before he found the location and marked it on the map. "That is less than ten kilometers south east of Biala Podlaska and the abandoned Polish Army training camp…" the Colonel said, suddenly frowning with suspicion.

The operator said nothing.

Colonel Stanyuta reached for a radio and snatched the microphone from its bracket. "Connect me with the Mechanized Brigade's intelligence officer."

He waited impatiently as the operator worked his complex radio equipment. The interior of the vehicle filled with a swirl of hissing static and then a double click as the call was connected.

"Major Gromyko," the Colonel spoke quickly. "What is the latest intelligence report we have on the Polish military camp at Biala Podlaska? Is it still abandoned as you assured me?"

There was a long moment of uncertain hesitation before the voice on the other end of the radio connection spoke, the tone muffled with echo. "Colonel, we have had no updates on the status of the Polish base since our Russian intelligence service update…"

"When was that, Gromyko?"

Another pause, this one somehow more troubled. "Six weeks ago, Colonel."

"What?" Stanyuta roared in a sudden fury. "How could we not be monitoring an enemy military base so close to the fucking border?"

"The… the Russians have been conducting the necessary intelligence surveillance on our behalf and liaising with our Headquarters staff at Minsk, Colonel."

"Fuck!" Colonel Stanyuta threw down the microphone and roared his frustration in the direction of the two hapless young radiomen trapped in the steel hull with him. "The fucking Russians! The fucking Russians, for God's sake! Their intel people are as lazy and as incompetent as our own!"

Stanyuta slumped down on the small padded bench and closed his eyes. His head ached, and he was weary and tormented by incompetence. He clawed at his temples with his fingers but the pounding inside his head only became more strident.

There were enemy troops at the Polish training base. He knew it now for a certainty. The only question remaining was how many men were there and how well were they equipped?

He had expected a clear run into Poland, at least as far as the city of Siedlce, before NATO would be able to muster a force sufficient to challenge the highway to Warsaw. Now he had an obstacle to overcome along the way. A minor one, to be sure, but still an unexpected delay to a timeline that was already several hours behind schedule.

"Fucking Russian liaison staff," he swore bitter contempt. "And fucking Army intelligence. Every one of the sons-of-whores should be put against a wall and shot."

Chapter 3:

The high wire gates at the Biala Podlaska military training base were wide open as Karl Armstrong and Charlie Mott approached in the bullet-riddled Ford Ranger.

The camp was a scene of frantic activity and rising alarm. Across the parade ground Polish soldiers were assembling into lines, kit bags and body armor were being stacked in untidy piles, and several Polish Army troop transport trucks were circling the barracks buildings, belching diesel fumes and kicking up clouds of dust. In the midst of the mayhem junior officers and NCOs were trying to shout their troops into orderly ranks, their barked orders adding to the sense of milling chaos.

"Seems like the Poles already know what's happening at the frontier," Charlie Mott understated. He cast a veteran's eye over the phalanx of rattled young Polish Army recruits and saw little to impress him.

Armstrong parked the Ford Ranger in front of the American Army barracks on the western side of the parade square and climbed down from the vehicle. He was full of urgent energy. "Charlie, get our boys assembled pronto. I want a meeting with all unit commanders in five minutes."

"I'll get on it."

"In the meantime, I'm going to see if any of our intelligence groups have a clear understanding of what's happening at the border and what's heading our way."

Armstrong strode towards his office and was met by adjutants and junior officers. The information coming into the base was fragmented. There had been reports from villagers around Terespol that Belarusian tanks were driving west, but so far there were no satellite intelligence images available and no first-hand reliable accounts of exactly what sized enemy force had crossed the border.

Armstrong listened to the updates, grim-faced and with a sense of rising frustration. The accounts amounted to a lot of speculation, a number of rumored sightings… but nothing definitive.

"Get on the horn to US Command at Warsaw and tell them we need satellite imagery of the Polish-Belarusian border between Brest and Bialystok," he insisted. "It's urgent. And tell them we need reconnaissance planes in the air."

No matter how loudly he shouted, Armstrong knew, any information from intelligence or recon sources was going to take several hours. He didn't have that time to spare.

He strode back across the parade ground. Major Mott and the rest of the detachment's command staff were standing in a huddle by the barracks door.

His command consisted of a full company of 173rd paratroopers and a company of combat engineers supported by eight unarmored M1297 A-GMV (Army-Ground Mobility Vehicles). Attached to those two infantry elements was an artillery battery of six M777 howitzers and their towing vehicles, as well as a Light Troop Scout Platoon of ten Humvees – five equipped with MK-19 grenade launchers, and the other five equipped with 50cal machine guns. For a training mission with Allied friendly troops, it was a well-rounded force. For a combat mission against an armored enemy, it was wholly inadequate.

"This is what we know for sure," Armstrong was a man who dealt in facts, not gossip. "A Platoon of Belarusian armored cars were sighted ten clicks southeast of here at dawn. They are a combat unit. They opened fire on Major Mott and me to attempt to prevent us reporting their location. That's all we know for sure. But there have been reports from Poles close to the border who claim Belarusian tanks have crossed the bridge at Brest and are on the highway, heading west towards Warsaw. We don't know if it's two tanks or two thousand. We don't know if they're supported by artillery or infantry. All we have right now is a whole lot of horse-shit and speculation."

The faces of the officers turned grave as they listened. Along the eastern skyline the sun was rising through a scar of black smoke, casting an ominous shadow over the army base and suggesting that, whatever the looming trouble, it was more significant than a single Platoon of enemy scout cars on a border crossing recce mission.

"The first thing we need is eyes on the ground," Armstrong insisted. "I want to know the nature of the attack, the makeup of the force in front of us, and whether it's just a probe by Belarusian scouts or a full-blown invasion of tanks and troops." He turned on the Captain commanding the Humvees. He was a young man with a square jaw, a nose that had been broken sometime in the past, and a buzz-cut of sandy hair. "Captain Roy, get your Cav boys mounted up. I want you to take a section of five vehicles east along the highway. Your mission is to find the enemy and observe. Understand?"

"Yes, sir," the young officer nodded. He was astonishingly elated at the prospect of action. He dashed across the parade ground, barking excited orders at his men as he raced towards the motor pool where the American Humvees were located.

"Stafford, I want those towed howitzers of yours hooked up to their FMTVs, ready to withdraw further west if we need to evacuate."

"Yes, sir," the Captain in command of 'Chaos' artillery battery nodded, tight-lipped and quietly fuming. His howitzers had been the centerpiece of the combined training program at the base, and his men had played a key part in tutoring the Polish infantry on how troops and artillery elements combined effectively in combat. Now, with the sudden prospect of a looming fight, his weapons were to be hitched to their trucks and spirited away without firing a shot in anger.

"I want the rest of the men ready in full battle rattle within fifteen minutes."

"What about the Polish troops, sir?" Charlie Mott prompted Armstrong.

Armstrong frowned. "I'm a Lieutenant Colonel in the 173rd. Our role here has been strictly training and advisory. I'm going to have to talk to Major Nowak and hope the man has a soldier's common sense…"

*

The Polish Battalion commander's office was on the northern side of the camp. When Karl Armstrong entered the building, the corridors were crammed with pale-faced adjutants milling in confusion. Armstrong shouldered his way through the open door into the main room and saw Major Nowak leaning over a large desk, his hands flat on the tabletop and a map of the frontier spread before him. Around the Major were his three Company Captains. Nowak's face was a dark scowl of concentration. He looked up and saw Armstrong's broad-shouldered frame in the doorway and his features lightened with momentary relief.

"I am glad you are here, Lieutenant Colonel Armstrong," the Polish officer muttered. He was a man in his fifties; a barrel-chested, squat-shaped figure with a face that had been scarred and pitted by childhood acne. His hair was grey, and his eyebrows were vast unruly bushes above thoughtful dark eyes. "You have heard the reports?"

"Some," Armstrong nodded. "Major Mott and I were fired upon by a Belarusian scouting unit of BRDM-2s ten clicks south east of here at dawn," he went on to quickly explain the morning's events. "They were well-armed and kitted out, Major."

Nowak wrenched his features into a pained expression. "We have been hearing from civilians along the frontier that several small communities were attacked overnight, the men killed and the women raped. Our border control points at Tersepol and Kukuryki are not responding to radio messages. My fear is the troops stationed at those places have been overrun, and now the bridges across the Bug are in Belarusian control."

"Well, if that's the case," Armstrong thought quickly, "it wouldn't be just for any kind of reconnaissance mission. We have to figure the Belarusians seized those bridges as part of an armored attack into Poland and that right now they have columns of MBTs and APCs on the road to Warsaw, and heading our way."

"Yes," Major Nowak drew a line across the map with his finger. "Biala Podlaska is on the route west to Warsaw. If the Belarusians plan on driving towards the capital, they will have to seize this city. We are straddling their path to the capital."

Lieutenant Colonel Armstrong frowned, confused. "Major, my intention is to evacuate my men west until we can ascertain exactly what sized enemy force we are up against. Surely you are not thinking of defending Biala Podlaska with just a Battalion of raw troops..."

The Polish officer flinched, stung by the American's incredulous tone. He raised himself to his full height, puffed out his chest and thrust his chin forward, his jaw clenched. "Certainly," he said with defiance. "We are proud Polish soldiers, Colonel Armstrong. If the Belarusians are invading our home, it is our duty to defend the Fatherland with our blood and with our lives, if necessary."

"But Major," Armstrong made an imploring appeal for reason, "We might be talking about an all-out invasion; hundreds of tanks, tens of thousands of infantry, and probably massed artillery with air support. You can't possibly hope to defend an entire city with a single Battalion of men."

"We can hold the enemy off and delay their advance..." Major Nowak insisted, "... with the help of your fine paratroopers, Colonel. And," he went on quickly, before Armstrong could interrupt, "we don't need to defend the city's outskirts to thwart the cursed invaders. All we need to do is deprive them of the facilities they need most."

The Polish officer stepped back from the table and turned to a wall-map that showed the city in detail. "Biala Podlaska is encircled by flat, featureless terrain. There are no hills and no high ground. Walls of forests and farm fields surround the city which is cut in half by the Krzna River that runs east to west. See?" he gestured for the American paratrooper to come closer. "The highway to Warsaw bypasses the northern outskirts and three main bridges link the north and south halves of the city. Those bridges are the key, Colonel Armstrong. On the southern side of the city are a train station and a disused airport. They are facilities the Belarusians will need to keep their Army supplied as it moves west! Deprive them of those key locations and we can hold up their advance until reinforcement troops can be rushed from Warsaw."

The Polish Major stepped back from the wall map and propped his hands on his hips. Armstrong studied the map more closely. "Can the abandoned runway accommodate heavy lift aircraft?" he asked around a grimace.

"Yes, probably," Nowak guessed.

Armstrong grunted; a sound like he had taken a punch to the guts. He lowered his head and stared at his boots for a long moment, deep in contemplative thought, then sighed his abdication. He could see the strategic importance of the train station and the airstrip. The enemy had to be denied those two key re-supply facilities at all costs. "Okay, Major," Armstrong muttered, heavy with the implications of his decision. "My men will help you defend the runway and train station until reinforcements arrive."

*

Karl Armstrong emerged into the gloomy morning light just as the column of five American M1025 Humvees commanded by Captain Roy were pulling out of the motor pool. Armstrong waved the lead vehicle down and the figure of the young officer appeared from behind the Kevlar-reinforced passenger door.

"Sir?" the young Captain looked fretful, worried that his chance at combat might be snatched away at the last moment. He was bristling with boyish enthusiasm at the prospect of battle. The five vehicles under his command were painted in woodlands camouflage colors, and each carried the dust, dents and scars of hard work. There was a man behind each Humvee's 50cal machine gun, standing thrust up through the roof hatch with dust goggles pulled down over their eyes.

"Hold up, Captain," Armstrong strode forward. "Change of plans. This is no longer a scouting mission – it's a delaying action to slow the enemy's advance and to measure their strength. I'm coming with you, and so is a Platoon of paratroopers armed with Javelins. Pull your vehicles over to the side of the main gates and wait for me there."

The five Humvees pulled to the edge of the parade ground, their engines idling. Armstrong went hunting for Major Mott and found his XO in the main barracks building.

"Charlie, we're going to defend Biala Podlaska with Major Nowak's Battalion of Polish infantry," he said simply. "There is an airstrip and a train station on the south bank of the city. We have to deny the Belarusians those two supply points until headquarters can rustle up some reinforcements." He saw the mortified look in his XOs eyes. It was a suicide mission.

"I know, I know," Armstrong waved Mott into silence before a protest could reach the man's lips. "But the decision has been made and now we have to make the best of it. I'm taking a Platoon of men east in the Humvees to scout the enemy, and hopefully slow the bastards down. I want you to work with the Poles to get every man and every piece of equipment evacuated to the southern bank of the city. There are three bridges that cross the river; that's going to be our first line of defense. I'll try to buy you some time to prepare a perimeter."

Charlie Mott nodded, fatalistic and grim-faced. Then he scowled. "Do you think you should be putting yourself in harm's way? Let me lead the Platoon."

"No dice," Armstrong rejected his XO's offer. "I need to see first-hand what we're up against. I want you to oversee the evacuation. And keep working the radios until I get back, for Christ's sake," Armstrong added as an afterthought. "We need to wake everyone in Warsaw up and get them moving on this. You know the drill and you know what has to be done. Make it happen."

"Okay," Mott nodded.

"I'll meet you at the bridges. Make sure everyone is dug in deep. We're going to stir up a hornet's nest in the next few hours, and by the time we return we're most likely going to have some angry enemy soldiers hard on our heels, understand?"

"What about the Abrams tanks?"

"The *what*?"

"The Abrams tanks," Mott prodded gently. "There are two Platoons of M1A2s on their way from Warsaw. They're supposed to arrive this morning, along with some VIPs. You were notified last night…"

"Oh, Christ!" Armstrong suddenly remembered the message his adjutant had handed him. He thought furiously for a second.

He needed those tanks!

Eight MBTs would add real steel to his plans to defend against the enemy's impending attack. "Tell the VIPs to turn around," Armstrong said. "Tell them they are heading into a potential war zone… and tell the Lieutenant commanding those Abrams to pull his thumb out of his backside and meet you at the Biala Podlaska bridges as quick as he can get here!"

Again, Mott nodded.

There was nothing more to be said; both men were experienced combat veterans. Fighting was their job, and they were uniquely skilled at their work.

When Armstrong re-emerged onto the parade ground, an adjutant was waiting for him with an armful of the Lieutenant Colonel's combat gear and his M4 rifle. Armstrong slipped the heavy body armor over his head and realized suddenly that he was still wearing denim jeans and his fishing shirt.

There was no time to change into his uniform.

"Okay, let's get going!" he took the M4 from the adjutant, made sure the weapon was loaded with a fresh magazine, and strode towards the lead Humvee. A Platoon of 173rd Sky Soldiers were clambering aboard the vehicles, including three two-man heavy weapons teams carrying FGM-148 Javelin CLUs and spare missiles. Armstrong climbed into the back of the overcrowded lead Humvee and raised his voice above the rumble of the engine.

"Move out!"

*

The five American Humvees joined the highway north of Biala Podlaska and sped east, driving in a column down a tree-lined avenue. To the left and right of the road stretched miles of flat farmland, sprinkled with small cottages and farmhouses. The morning seemed sleepily tranquil; the road was abandoned and the windows on the houses they passed remained tightly shuttered.

Ahead of the convoy and still far over the horizon, a dark cloud of smoke boiled into the sky, brooding and black with menace.

Armstrong studied the faces of the men crammed close around him as the Humvees raced towards danger. The paratroopers at his side looked absurdly young, their expressions tight with apprehension. They were all highly-trained professionals, but few had seen combat action. So far their young careers had consisted mainly of relentless military exercises that could never, Armstrong knew well, adequately replicate the sheer terror and chaos of a firefight against an armed enemy. The soldiers sat, feigning casual indifference, and it was only the hectic fretful look in their eyes that betrayed their rising anxiety.

The convoy approached a hamlet consisting of a dozen stone houses and buildings on either side of the highway, and an intersection south. The Humvees blew through the crossing at high speed. Beyond the last buildings the surrounding terrain changed to dark stretches of forested land that pressed close to the road for several miles. The Humvees pulled to the shoulder of the road and the paratroopers climbed down into the dirt.

"This is where we'll fight them," Armstrong announced. He turned a slow circle to study the topography. The land was flat and the trees grew so close together that their foliage formed an overhead canopy of deep leafy shadow. The ground was carpeted in bushy undergrowth that would conceal an ambush from an unsuspecting enemy until the very last minute. He walked the length of the highway for several hundred yards, studying the gravel shoulders of the road on both sides with Captain Roy and the Lieutenant in command of the Platoon of paratroopers following him.

"This forest is going to force the enemy to funnel into a tight column," Armstrong reached a kink in the road and stopped suddenly. He turned his head and guessed the distance back to the waiting Humvees; about five hundred yards.

"When they round this bend, they're going to be blind to what's ahead of them. They'll come around the corner at high speed, but once we open fire on the lead tanks, they'll be hemmed in by the trees on either side."

Captain Roy nodded.

"So…" Armstrong drew a deep breath and bent his mind to the tactical situation. The plan developed quickly in his imagination as he visualized the enemy's approach and calculated their most probable reactions. "… I want a two-man OP set up a mile further down the road," Armstrong turned to the Lieutenant commanding the paratroopers. "Give them a radio and tell them to report to me the moment they see the enemy approach."

The Lieutenant nodded.

"And I want the 50cal machine guns unattached from your Humvees, Captain Roy, and brought forward. Set them up there and there," he pointed to the side of the road from where the heavy machineguns could enfilade the highway. "We'll never get our vehicles into those dense woods and out again in a hurry. So, park the Humvees back at the hamlet, out of the way, and have them ready for us to evacuate if everything goes to hell."

Captain Roy pulled a notepad from his pocket and jotted notes, his brow furrowed with concentration. Dismounting the 50cals would be a bitch; each weapon weighed around ninety pounds and the tripod another thirty. Carrying the cans of ammunition would require a third man. All in all, it was a bastard of a job – and the retrograde movement back to the Humvees, if they were under enemy fire, would be a nightmare.

"Sir," Roy interrupted boldly. "How about we dismount one 50cal and take some M240 machine guns with armor-piercing rounds forward instead? I'm thinking of the difficulties of an exfil under enemy fire…"

Armstrong thought for a moment and nodded his head. "Okay. Make it so. And
I want to locate the Javelins well back from the bend," the Colonel went on. "We need the enemy's tanks completely committed to this stretch of road before we open fire. And I want the rest of your Platoon, Lieutenant, in foxholes on either side of the road ahead of them. Once the Javelins open fire, the enemy will most likely try to bring up infantry to clear the highway. We need to be ruthless, gentlemen. Between the Javelins, the 50cals and our Platoon fire, we need to make the enemy pay a high price for this piece of road, understand?"

*

"Six-Six, One-Two," the men in the observation post had direct radio comms with Armstrong. "Enemy in sight. Estimate at least Mechanized Brigade strength T-72 MBTs supported by flanking columns of APCs." The two paratroopers had concealed themselves in the roof of a barn that was set well back from the highway and over a mile further east of the Platoon's ambush position. From their elevated perch in a clearing on the far side of the forest they had an unobstructed view of the Belarusian armored spearhead as it steamrolled west ahead of a billowing cloud of swirling dust.

The tanks were speeding along the highway in columns of Companies with echelons of squat BMP-2s in the fields on either flank.

"Roger, One-Two," Armstrong set the radio aside and passed the word to Captain Roy and the paratrooper

Lieutenant. The officers spread the word to their waiting men while Karl Armstrong took a long reflective moment to consider his own emotions.

He was relieved; he had not known until this very moment whether the Belarusian push across the border was part of a provocative probe or a full-scale invasion. Now he knew, and he felt vindicated for taking pre-emptive measures to face the threat head-on. He was also secretly anxious. He had pleaded for an opportunity to join the war and fight on the front lines of battle. Now the war had found him.

Would he measure up?

Suddenly Armstrong's Afghanistan experiences seemed a long time in the past, and the Belarusian military would prove a sterner test of his mettle than the enemies he had encountered in the blazing desert heat.

He stared down at his hands that gripped the M4. He could feel his fingers trembling and the realization enraged him.

Man up, and do your fuckin' job, Karl Armstrong berated himself cruelly. *Shit is about to get real, and it's time for you to walk the walk…*

*

The highway west was two lanes wide and the Belarusian T-72 tanks in the vanguard of the invasion force went forward, driving down the middle of the blacktop with the commanders of each vehicle standing upright in their turrets, their silhouetted figures partially protected by each tank's open hatch cover.

The attack was nine hours behind schedule and slipping even further behind by the minute. Now, immediately ahead of them, stood a dense palisade of forest, necessitating a change in formation. The flanking echelons of BMP-2s slowed to allow the first Battalion of tanks to move forward, and then the APCs folded in behind the last tank in the formation until the entire attack column was strung out in single file stretching several miles back down the cluttered road.

Alerted to the delay at the spearhead of the invasion force, Colonel Stanyuta chafed in fuming frustration, barking orders from his command vehicle. He was parked on the shoulder of the road three miles behind the leading tanks and cursing bitterly at each fresh delay.

"Keep those tanks rolling!" he demanded. "Don't stop for anything. Move! Move! Move!" he bellowed across the net.

The first Company of T-72s trundled forward, picking up speed as they approached a gentle turn in the road. The commander in the lead vehicle studied the map in his hand as his tank accelerated. The next waypoint on their advance was a small hamlet, about a kilometer to the west. He dropped the map down inside the turret and snatched for the binoculars slung around his neck. His driver swerved suddenly, throwing the commander off balance. He cursed the fool under his breath and steadied the binoculars on the tiled rooftops in the distance. The buildings were at the end of a long straight stretch of road, hemmed in on both sides by a wall of tall forest trees. The road ahead was draped in deep shadow, the highway criss-crossed with muddy tire tracks and still damp from overnight dew.

"Driver. Faster," the T-72 commander spoke across the tank's radio.

The three American Javelin teams were in hastily-dug shallow foxholes at the far end of the highway. The operators had their CLUs to their shoulders, a missile already loaded and the systems powered up, waiting only to be triggered into action. Karl Armstrong lay positioned half-way along the highway with a handful of paratroopers, their weapons locked and loaded. They were concealed twenty yards into the fringe of the forest, stretched prone in the wet undergrowth. The first enemy tank trundled past Armstrong's hiding place, its grinding steel wheels and tracks thick with clumps of mud.

Armstrong counted down the seconds. Another enemy tank sped past his position and then a third. "Come on!" he urged the Javelin operators under his breath. "Open fire!"

The first Javelin operator set the weapon for a soft launch to help conceal his position, then pushed the ATTK SEL switch on the right handgrip of his CLU to change attack modes from the default 'Top Attack' to 'Direct Attack'. The lead Belarusian T-72 was just a few hundred yards from his firing position and closing the distance quickly. The operator's index finger felt for the fire trigger on the front side of the right handgrip and he squeezed…

The Javelin missile leaped from the launch tube and streaked low across the sky; the path of its trajectory dazzlingly bright in the dark shadowy gloom. It struck the lead T-72 flush on the front hull and exploded in a thunderclap of fire and smoke.

Armstrong heard the wicked *'crack!'* as the missile detonated. The ground beneath him rumbled and then the road became engulfed in a billow of black boiling smoke and the urgent whine of heavy engines.

The second T-72 was following so closely, and at such speed, that the driver had no time to react. The tank slammed into the rear of the lead vehicle, then slewed sideways towards the fringe of trees. The second Javelin team opened fire on the hapless Belarusian T-72, and the missile made a direct hit, smashing through the side armor and exploding; killing the three-man crew and engulfing the stricken steel beast in roaring flames.

"Driver! Hard left!" the commander in the third T-72 saw the blazing twisted horror ahead of him and his voice cracked with panic. The driver responded to the shouted order, swishing the tank deftly clear of the carnage and onto the shoulder of the highway. The operator of the third Javelin team squeezed the trigger on his CLU at the same moment the swerving T-72 burst through the billowing smoke and lurched back onto the road. The missile streaked across the ground and struck the enemy tank's domed turret, killing the commander instantly and rendering the vehicle helpless. Fire leaped from the sprung turret hatch and the cries of men burning alive inside the steel coffin carried on the morning air to the trenches where the American paratroopers lay concealed. The ghastly sound was a torturous torment as the Belarusian crewmen were slowly incinerated.

With the first three T-72s destroyed the highway was effectively barricaded by twisted burning steel. The following tanks in the column were forced to pull to the shadow-struck shoulder of the road, their turret-slaved coax machine guns aimed into the surrounding forest and firing in a blaze of blind panic.

It took a well-trained team just thirty seconds to reload a Javelin weapon system. The Sky Soldiers of the 173rd Airborne Brigade were amongst the best-drilled troops in the world.

The first Javelin team fired thirty-five seconds after their initial missile had blasted from the launch tube. The highway had become a target-rich environment. The Belarusian tanks were log-jammed along the length of the highway behind a haze of drifting smoke. The operator fired the missile in 'Top Attack' mode and it went streaking away into the sky on a thin feather of exhaust smoke, then plunged down into the milling chaos further along the highway, spearing through the thin top armor of another T-72 and blowing the vehicle to pieces. The tank seemed to sag on its suspension for a split second and then exploded outwards in a huge tower of flames and roiling smoke. Metal fragments were torn from the tangled carcass and flung hundreds of yards into the surrounding trees.

The Belarusian Captain commanding the Company of tanks frantically ordered two of his stranded T-72s to barge their way through the mangled wreckage to clear the highway. The MBTs nosed forward into the smoke and flames and began to shunt one of the destroyed vehicles towards the fringe of woods. Another Javelin team fired in 'Direct Attack' mode and in the blink of an eye a withering white streak of light flashed along the highway. The nearest T-72 was struck broadside by the Javelin missile, destroying the tank's left-side roadwheels. The three-man crew bailed out of the stricken vehicle into the chaos and fiery mayhem. The commander's uniform caught alight and he became engulfed in flames, staggering and screaming in the center of the blacktop. The gunner and driver reached the shoulder of the road but were cut down by a spray of automatic rifle fire from an alert paratrooper. The driver died instantly, shot through the chest. The gunner took a bullet in his torso and curled up in the mud, his body tucked into a tight ball and his hands clamped over the gaping wound until he bled out.

The Belarusian tank column devolved into a milling calamity of confusion. Then, into the smoke and chaos, a dozen BMP-2 armored fighting vehicles appeared. They swarmed down the gravel shoulder of the highway, weaving a ragged path around the stalled tank column.

The BMP-2 was a product of the Soviet-era 1980s. The tracked vehicle featured the same hull as its predecessor, the BMP-1, however, carried a larger two-man conical turret that mounted three separate weapons systems; a 30mm 2A42 dual-feed autocannon, a coaxial 7.62mm PKT machine gun and a cylindrical ATGM launcher capable of firing the AT-4 'Spigot' missile. Each vehicle was crewed by three men and carried seven infantrymen in their steel hulls.

The vehicles reached the mangled wreckage of the destroyed tanks with their machine guns blazing wild suppressing fire into the fringes of the woods. They popped off a dense cloud of smoke to conceal their positions and then the two doors in the hull's rear opened and the infantry spilled out into the mud. In a matter of seconds, a full Company of Belarusian troops were at the edge of the forest, armed and adding their own frantic suppressing fire to the hammering crescendo.

"Open fire!" Karl Armstrong bellowed and the fringe of the woods lit up with pinpricks of flickering flame and the roar of automatic weapons. Streaks of light flashed through the gloomy forest as the concealed paratroopers picked their targets and began the ruthless slaughter.

The 50cal machine gun and the M240s added their throaty thumping roar to the fury, targeting the vulnerable side and rear armor of the closest enemy BMPs. The range was less than two hundred yards and the heavy-hitting impact of the machine guns tore the lead Belarusian vehicle to shreds, killing the driver. The BMP caught fire and billowed black choking smoke from its open rear doors. The surviving crewmen bailed out of the wreck and were cut down by a swathe of American light arms fire as they attempted to scramble for cover.

The noise of the firefight was deafening. M4s cracked incessantly, Belarusian HMG fire whipsawed through the trees, grenades exploded, and underscoring it all were the shouts and screams of men dying in agony. A Belarusian infantry Lieutenant was struck by paratrooper fire as he was marshaling his men for an assault into the forest. The impact of the bullets flung the man back, throwing him hard against the steel hull of a BMP. A young soldier went to his officer's aid, dragging his deadweight through the gravel and mud into shelter, and leaving a wet stain of bright red blood across the blacktop. A grenade sailed through the air, thrown from the roadside. It clattered against a tree and ricocheted to the ground then exploded in a flash of light and upheaved earth. A bullet whipped past Karl Armstrong's face as he was aiming to fire. Another thwacked into the earthen lip of his foxhole. On either side of Armstrong, the rest of the paratroopers were firing with calm practiced composure, husbanding their ammunition, firing single rounds and making each one count. Further along the line, and closer to where the two 50cals were located, the enemy were gathering in small knots behind the steel shelter of their stalled tanks, preparing to charge the American positions.

Armstrong fired his M4 at the silhouette of a Belarusian officer who stood shouting orders to the men around him. The shot missed, but struck one of the nearby infantrymen in the shoulder. He put a second bullet into the tight knot of men and again missed the Belarusian officer, wounding the same man he had just shot a second time. He cursed his poor marksmanship bitterly.

Armstrong knew he could not hold contact with the enemy and allow the battle to develop into a prolonged firefight. The Americans had the element of surprise and the advantage of soft cover, but those factors would not last for long. Once the Belarusians brought up more infantry and additional heavy weapons support, the paratrooper positions would be overwhelmed. He raised his M4, changing aim. He spotted an enemy infantryman running through the fringe of the woods and fired. The enemy soldier went down, shot in the chest, the impact of the bullet punching the man clean off his feet.

"Thirty seconds!" Armstrong shouted to the men in foxholes on either side of him. "Thirty seconds then exfil!"

The paratroopers seemed to redouble the fury of their fire, picking off enemy soldiers before they could reach the shadowed margin of the trees. It was a massacre. The Belarusians were caught exposed on the open road and were savagely cut down.

"Go! Go! Go!" Armstrong shouted at two paratroopers to his left. They leaped from cover and ran, doubled-over, deeper into the trees then began circling back towards the hamlet where the Humvees were waiting. Element by element, the Americans dissolved into the gloom, while the surviving enemy troops from that first furious fusillade cowered close to the shelter of their armored vehicles and continued to fire wildly into the trees through the swirling haze of smoke.

Two paratroopers were hit during the exfil. Both men killed outright by Belarusian machine gun fire. The surviving paratroopers evacuated their positions behind several smoke grenades and dissolved into the misted shadows of the forest, circling back to the hamlet. Behind them enemy fire still blazed erratically into the deserted woods.

Karl Armstrong was amongst the last men to arrive at the village. He was lathered in sweat and still pumped full of adrenaline. He ordered the bodies of the two dead men lifted reverently into the rear of the first Humvee and then the rest of the Americans piled aboard the overcrowded vehicles. Armstrong was the last man to board. He was assessing the action and processing his own emotions. The ambush had been well executed and had served two purposes; it had put a dent in the enemy's strength and it had warned the Belarusians that from this point on the road west would be contested – forcing the enemy to proceed with debilitating caution. Armstrong was satisfied – and he felt vindicated. He had craved a chance for combat yet he had agonized too, whether he would measure up to the challenge.

Now he had the answer.

In the terrifying cauldron of chaos and clamor he had emerged steady and undaunted.

Chapter 4:

The encrypted phone on the leather seat beside him rang and General Chris Buford snatched for it.

"SACEUR," the USAF Four-star General answered. He was the Supreme Allied Commander Europe; the man responsible for NATOs defense against the Russians. Ever since NATO's inception in the 1950s, an American military officer had always filled the role of SACEUR – beginning with Dwight D. Eisenhower. Buford was the latest in a long and distinguished line of illustrious military leaders – and the first to be confronted with the horror of a World War.

Buford listened, while through the tinted windows of the black armored BMW, the Belgian landscape flashed by. He was a tall, lean man with greying hair and a hawk-like nose. He waited until the caller had finished speaking and then cursed quietly under his breath.

Buford threw the phone down and trapped his bottom lip between his teeth, thinking quickly. He flicked a glance sideways to where his NATO aide sat with a stack of folders resting in his lap.

"Order the car to turn around," he told his aide. "I need to get back to SHAPE as quickly as possible. And start working the phones. I want everyone important assembled in the CCOMC within one hour. The Belarusians have just invaded central Poland. They moved tanks and troops across the bridges at Brest and Kukuryki overnight and now they're driving headlong west towards Warsaw as we speak."

*

The column of Humvees turned off the highway at Biala Podlaska and raced south along the city's main thoroughfare. They reached a busy intersection and blew through the traffic lights without stopping. The northbound lanes leading out of the city were jammed with bumper-to-bumper traffic; civilians with their cars crammed full of family possessions evacuating their homes. There was a sense of panic and frantic urgency across the city; car horns blared and the sidewalks were crowded.

The Humvees crossed an overpass that spanned a narrow steam and ran headlong into the column of Army trucks that had evacuated the troops from the training base. The Humvees pulled to the side of the road by a gas station. Major Mott stood on the opposite side of the road in an overgrown field looking north. Karl Armstrong climbed down from the Humvee and strode across the road. He had a sick sliding sensation in the pit of his guts. He glanced towards the stream with an aghast sense of loathing.

"Charlie… don't tell me…"

"I'm afraid so," Charlie Mott made an anguished face. "You're looking at the Krzna River."

"Jesus H. Christ!" Armstrong cursed. He strode through the grass to the reed-strewn bank and swore vehemently and bitterly. The Krzna was a stream with shallow grassy banks, no more than twenty feet wide that meandered lazily through the surrounding tree-studded fields. "That's not a fucking river!" Armstrong seethed. He turned his head. The causeway they had crossed, he assumed, was one of the 'bridges' Major Nowak had insisted the paratroopers defend. It was nothing but a short stretch of two-lane road with steel handrails on either side.

"The other bridges…?" Armstrong asked with a grimace.

"The same," Charlie Mott delivered the bad news. "The next crossing is beyond that bend, about six hundred yards to the east," he pointed. "The third crossing is another five hundred further on."

"Sonofabitch!"

The three crossings were indefensible. The Belarusians could bring up bridging equipment and span the Krzna anywhere within two miles of where the men stood with just a couple of lengths of steel ribbon bridge in less than fifteen minutes.

"Tell me it gets better," Karl Armstrong clawed his hands through his hair and pondered the depths of his dilemma.

"A little," Charlie Mott said. "We managed to reach U.S. Command in Warsaw. They're in touch with NATO in Belgium. Headquarters is aware of the Belarusian invasion and we're standing by to hear when and how we will be reinforced. And the Abrams tanks we are expecting will be here in about twenty minutes. I just got off the radio with the Lieutenant in command. He's high-tailing it at best speed."

Armstrong grunted. "Thank God for small mercies," he grumbled. "Let's hope Command moves fast, Charlie, because there's at least a full-strength Belarusian Mechanized Brigade on the highway east of here and closing on our position; T-72s, APCs and no doubt a whole shit-load of heavy artillery."

Suddenly Major Mott took in Armstrong's appearance, noting the mud and the blood spatters on the Colonel's clothes. His voice lowered with concern. "We heard the fighting," he said somberly. "Casualties?"

"Two dead," Armstrong pointed back across the road where the Platoon of paratroopers were dismounting from the Humvees bearing blanket-draped corpses. The soldiers were filthy with dust and mud and blood, moving with the bone-weary heaviness of old men.

Death was an inevitable consequence of war, but that knowledge did not make the grave news any easier to accept. Mott and Armstrong lapsed into introspective quiet for several long seconds – until the roaring engine of an approaching Ford Ranger broke the respectful tribute to their fallen comrades.

Major Nowak climbed down from the 4WD and hitched up his trousers with his hands as he strode through the long grass. He was wearing full combat gear; the sidearm belted around his waist hanging low off his hip like a wild west gunslinger. He moved with long purposeful strides, his features working in agitation as he drew closer. He was broad-shouldered and a little overweight. His fleshy face glistened with a sheen of sweat.

"Colonel Armstrong, you contacted the enemy? Can you give me a report?"

Armstrong was in no mood for détente or pleasantries. He eyed the Polish Major with scorn. "You bullshitted me," he fired off the first shot and saw the Polish officer's stride falter. "You told me these river crossings could be defended. Well, they can't. They're not bridges, and this is not a fucking river."

The Polish Major bristled. "I am a proud Pole," he thrust out his chin. "I and all my men have sworn to lay down our lives in defense of the Fatherland. I did only what I deemed necessary to that end."

"Yeah, well in doing so, Major, you've put every one of my men's lives at risk. A few miles to the east of here is an enemy Mechanized Brigade swarming across the countryside like a plague of locusts. In an hour from now they're going to be on the city's outskirts," Armstrong seethed. "Instead of us evacuating to a place that can be defended, you've committed us to a hellish landscape that's about to be soaked in blood. I hope your pride is worth the price my men are about to pay."

*

The next thirty minutes disappeared in a flurry of barked orders and frantic activity. The six M777 howitzers of 'Chaos' Battery were set up on the grassy verge of a shopping center parking lot and the paratroopers were allocated defensive responsibilities for the two most-westerly crossings, leaving the eastern bridge to Major Nowak's full Battalion of Polish infantry. Armstrong set up his headquarters in a run-down apartment block beside the main road from where he had an elevated view of all three crossing points.

The American Colonel was waiting impatiently for his headquarters staff to establish comms links between the troops stationed at each crossing when the sudden unmistakable rumble of approaching heavy vehicles carried on the fitful breeze. Armstrong crossed to the nearest window and stared north. A convoy of eight M1A2 Abrams tanks rounded a tree-lined bend in the road and raced towards the river.

He watched the MBTs cross the Krzna and then park in a nearby field. The paratroopers digging trenches along the riverbank gave the arriving tanks a ragged cheer.

Armstrong swarmed down the stairs and strode across the road. The commander in the lead Abrams climbed out of the vehicle through his turret hatch and leaped lightly to the ground.

He was a young man with flaming orange hair, pale skin, and a face full of freckles. He stepped forward to meet Armstrong by the roadside and saluted. "Lieutenant Jim Grimsby, sir."

"Glad to have you here, soldier," Armstrong returned the salute. The Colonel gave the tanker a quick sitrep and then the conversation became an intense discussion about the role the Abrams would play in defending each river crossing. Two tanks would help defend each bridge and the last two MBTs would be kept in reserve at the abandoned airstrip. The Abrams had arrived without their normal support vehicles. The only ammunition they had was what they carried aboard the tanks.

Typically, Abrams tanks carried different ammunition loadouts depending on their mission. The two platoons had stowed a mixture of sabot and the Army's new AMP round. The 120mm AMP (Advance Multi-purpose) had a sophisticated fusing system that allowed the munition to perform differently to match a variety of targets. The AMP replaced the traditional HEAT and Canister rounds, and was effective against light armored vehicles, obstacles, bunkers and personnel.

After several minutes a Humvee appeared at the far end of the street and came barreling over the Krzna. The vehicle braked to a skidding halt on the shoulder of the blacktop. The Humvee's passenger door was flung open and a beautiful dark-haired young woman stepped down from the vehicle. She was wearing a white shirt and tight denim jeans. Her eyes were hidden behind Aviator sunglasses. She strode towards Armstrong, and on her red lipsticked lips was a dazzling smile.

"Colonel?" her voice was throaty and sensual. "My name is Janna Vidas. I'm a journalist with CMM. I've come from Warsaw with my cameraman to film news reports for our viewers back in America. I understand your headquarters told you to expect a couple of VIPs and that you will afford me every cooperation…"

*

The expressions on the faces of the NATO officers assembled in the CCOMC (Comprehensive Crisis Operations Management Center) at SHAPE headquarters outside Mons, Belgium, reflected the bleakness of the situation.

General Chris Buford sat at the head of the table with his Deputy (DSACEUR) at his right. General Sir Walter Fisk was a British Army Officer who had served with distinction in Bosnia, Iraq and Afghanistan.

It was Fisk who opened the meeting, providing a summary of the crisis in central Poland. "Under the cover of darkness last night, a Mechanized Brigade of Belarusian troops and armor seized the bridges at Brest and Kukuryki and made a concerted push into central Poland, killing and committing atrocities indiscriminately," the British officer gave the dry bare facts. "We believe there may be more enemy troops massing in Belarus to support the invasion, but at this moment it is the advance of the Mechanized Brigade already in-country we must deal with. Satellite coverage is problematic because US Intelligence services are focused on the Russian Armies along the Lithuanian frontier, so the only reports we're getting from eastern central Poland right now are first-hand."

"What do we have to put in the way of the Belarusians?" a high-ranking German officer attached to NATO asked. He was seated at the far end of the table; his hands clasped tightly together on the tabletop like an attentive school student.

"Bugger all, actually," Fisk said with disarming British frankness. "We have two companies of 173rd Airborne Brigade paratroopers and a Battalion of Polish infantry. They have been conducting joint training exercises at a camp close to the border. Latest word has them preparing to defend the city of Biala Podlaska with a couple of Platoons of Abrams tanks that, by coincidence, were on their way to cooperate in the training mission when the Belarusians surged over the frontier."

"And that's all?" the German officer looked wide-eyed with alarm.

"I'm afraid so," Fisk said.

"And there's not a hell of a lot we can muster, either," Buford picked up the thread of the discussion. "The Americans are weeks away from arriving in Europe in force, the British and Germans are only now beginning to mobilize, and all we have in-country are Polish units and the remnants of the NATO eFP Battle Group that was crushed in the Baltics. Those troops are arrayed around the Suwalki Gap. At short notice we can maybe rustle up some American bombers and some French, German and British fighters."

"Aircraft won't win a ground war," a Canadian officer at the long table stated the obvious. "We need men on the ground. If the Belarusians aren't stopped, they'll roll all the way to Warsaw… and the Russians will be there to meet them."

The bleak reality was that NATO forces were stretched threadbare and would continue to be for several weeks.

"There is one option…" the German officer lifted his head suddenly as a wild idea took shape in his imagination. "We could send the rest of the 173rd Airborne Brigade. They're the European Command's conventional airborne strategic response force in Europe."

The 173rd was based in Vincenza, Italy, on twenty-four-hour standby. They were an elite force of paratroopers who bore the burden of being an urgent response force to a developing crisis.

"They're an IBCT," (Infantry Brigade Combat Team) Buford shook his head. "They're not going to be able to deal with a mechanized enemy of tanks and armored personnel carriers."

The German officer's face turned dark and cruel. "They'll have to," he said. "Because we have no other choice. If the 173rd can't stop the Belarusians, then Warsaw and Poland will fall within seven days and Russia will have won the war."

Buford sat back in his chair, deeply troubled. He was caught between a rock and a hard place. To do nothing was to surrender western Europe to the Russians with barely a fight… but to send the 173rd Sky Soldiers into battle against an enemy with hundreds of MBTs and armored personnel carriers was akin to a suicide mission.

He glanced sideways at Walter Fisk and saw his own misgivings reflected in the face of his Deputy. Buford sighed and for a long moment the glass-walled room was draped in doom-laden silence.

"How long will it take to mobilize the 173rd?" SACEUR asked Fisk. "How long before we can have them in the air over central Poland?"

The British officer didn't know the accurate answer to that question. "I'll make some phone calls," he said. "But, at a guess, weather over the combat zone permitting, I'd say eighteen hours from when you give the word…"

Chris Buford nodded. "Issue the order," he made the decision. "Tell the 173rd they're going into harm's way. Then get on the radio to the troops defending Biala Podlaska. Tell them they have to hold up the Belarusian invasion at all costs for eighteen hours until help arrives."

*

For long unholy moments of disbelief, Karl Armstrong stared at the female journalist. He recognized her immediately from the television report the previous evening. "You were contacted by radio this morning by my Executive Officer and given explicit instructions to return to Warsaw," he snapped, his temper suffusing his face with red burning color. "You've driven straight into a god-damned war zone. You have to evacuate immediately."

He plucked at Janna Vidas' elbow and steered her back towards the Humvee. She tugged away and turned on him, her slanted blue eyes sparking fury. She stood on the verge of the road with her hands clenched on her hips and her lip curled in a stubborn snarl of defiance.

"I and my cameraman have permission to be here!" she glared "My network made the arrangements with your headquarters."

"I don't care if the goddamned President of the United States signed the paperwork," Karl Armstrong raged. "Any minute now the road you just arrived on is going to be swarming with enemy tanks and infantry. A lot of people are going to die, and I don't need some bleeding-heart journalist in the way while I'm trying to do my job!"

"I'm here to do *my* job, Colonel!"

Armstrong's lips pressed tight into a pale, furious line. "Look, lady. You might be an important TV personality and a champion of the liberal media, but that counts for nothing here. Bullets don't give a damn about your virtue or your righteousness." He stared at her, his face cold and set.

"And I don't care about the danger," she retorted hotly. "I'm a professional journalist. My cameraman and I have been in conflict zones before so I'm staying right here unless my network tells me otherwise… and I *am* going to report on this war, Colonel, – whether you like it or not!"

*

The tide of refugees streamed north and west along every road out of Biala Podlaska. As the lead elements of the Belarusian invasion force approached the outskirts sporadic gunfire broke out and the mass of miserable humanity broke into wild panic.

The gunfire carried clearly to the southern suburbs of the city where the Americans and Polish were frantically preparing to defend the riverbank. High overhead two Belarusian Army

Burevestnik-MB fixed-wing UAVs circled the smoke-stained sky, spying on the Allied positions.

Four miles east of the city's outskirts, parked in a clearing by the side of the highway, Colonel Stanyuta watched the live feed from the drones with keen interest, noting the unexpected presence of several American Abrams tanks with a dark troubled scowl.

He strode back to his command vehicle. A uniformed aide handed the Colonel a hot bowl of borscht and a chunk of dark bread. Stanyuta ate ravenously and then spoke at length by radio to his artillery commander. Most of the Army's towed artillery pieces were stranded many miles behind the tanks and APCs, lumbering along the highway behind heavy lorries. They would not reach the outskirts of Biala Podlaska until late in the afternoon. However, there were several batteries of BM-21A BelGrad (Belorussian Grad) multiple rocket launchers on the road, mounted aboard MAZ-6317 6x6 heavy utility trucks. Stanyuta ordered the highway cleared and the rocket launchers escorted urgently forward to the battlefront.

The BM-21A BelGrad had been developed by the Belarusian military to replace an aging Soviet predecessor. The new weapons system mounted a phalanx of forty launching tubes for 122mm rockets.

"The enemy have fixed themselves to the southern bank of the Krzna River," Major Gromyko, the Belarusian Army intelligence officer, made his official report to the Colonel. It was nothing Stanyuta had not already seen for himself on the live feed from the circling drones. "There are probably two Battalions of infantry and a handful of enemy tanks defending the perimeter. They shouldn't hold us up for more than an hour," Gromyko finished his analysis of the video feeds with a confident prediction and then flashed the Colonel a grin of imminent triumph.

"You think so?" Colonel Stanyuta grunted acidly and then turned on the officer. "Look again more closely at your drone feed, Gromyko. Some of those men are American paratroopers. They are the enemy troops who were stationed at the training camp you didn't tell me about," he snarled, prodding the Intelligence officer in the chest with his finger. "The same arrogant American bastards who shot up my column of T-72s this morning with their Javelin fucking missiles! Now you're telling me they won't slow our attack for more than an hour? We should have seized the fucking airport and the train station eight hours ago – and we would have if your intelligence had been more thorough. Now, because of your incompetence, we have an unexpected enemy of American elite airborne soldiers to deal with."

*

Three batteries of BM-21A BelGrad multiple rocket launchers fired their first salvo at the Allied positions along the Krzna River a few minutes after noon. The storm of rockets shrieked across the sky and plunged to earth in a howling torment of thunderous horror.

A handful of the rockets struck buildings on the northern bank of the river, destroying homes, offices and hotels. Straggling refugees, burdened by the weight of their belongings, were cut down and slaughtered. The sky lit with fireballs of flames and columns of black boiling smoke, and the ground trembled with each fresh thunderclap of roaring noise. A woman screamed because her young son was flung down dead in the gutter, his body mangled by shrapnel. A man dragging his dog by a leash was eviscerated into bloody gore, leaving the animal untouched. A family sedan, stalled on the roadside, was immolated in flames, incinerating everyone inside the vehicle in a flash of searing light.

Janna Vidas and her cameraman were preparing to interview a fear-stricken Polish woman on a street corner south of the river when the sky suddenly filled with streaking grey contrails of smoke and the menace of inbound rockets.

Vidas was wearing a flak-jacket over her shirt, calming the wailing woman as her cameraman set up the shot. Tavish 'Tosh' Kennedy was a hard-drinking chain-smoking Scot who had fled his native Glasgow for America a decade earlier. He had a Spielberg-like talent for cinematic drama. He stepped off the sidewalk and into the street so the camera could pick up the darkening smoke-filled sky to the north with a wide shot. He gave the journalist a 'thumbs-up' and Vidas turned to the camera, her face instantly composed into a troubled expression as she began her introduction.

Suddenly three deafeningly loud explosions shook the ground. Vidas turned towards the sound and saw an apartment block less than a hundred yards from where she was standing vaporized. The entire building dissolved in a flash of fire and an almighty roar of noise. A hail of debris fell from the sky; chunks of masonry and broken bricks flung like shrapnel. The magnitude of the explosion was quake-like, hurling Vidas and Kennedy to the ground. The Polish woman was crushed to death by a crumbling wall.

Vidas scrambled unsteadily to her feet, horror-stricken. She was spattered in fresh blood and grey with dust and ash. She gaped wide-eyed at the debris and saw the broken figure of the Polish woman buried in the ruins.

A minute of shocked eerie silence passed. Kennedy got to his feet and checked the camera. He had a cut over his right eye and blood running down his cheek. He took three staggering steps towards Janna Vidas and then another salvo of inbound Belarusian rockets came plunging down through the swirling clouds of smoke. Vidas lifted her head in bewilderment. For an instant the world seemed strangely quiet and then a deafening explosion split the silence apart. It sounded like an avalanche; a cacophony of ear-splitting chaos followed by a fireball of flame. A wave of searing heat blasted over her.

"Jesus Christ!" Karl Armstrong was standing at the window of his commandeered headquarters building watching the fall of enemy rockets as they rained down on the riverbank. When he turned to the south, he saw Janna Vidas standing on a street corner amidst a tangle of twisted debris.

Armstrong swarmed down the stairs bellowing for two aides to follow him. He dashed south along a narrow side street, weaving like a running back between fallen mountains of debris and shattered glass, seething with outrage and fury. He reached the street corner ten paces ahead of his aides, shouting as he ran.

"Get down!" he bellowed at the journalist. "Get down on the ground!"

Janna Vidas turned towards the bark of Armstrong's voice just as another Belarusian rocket struck the intersection. The explosion blew out the windows of the surrounding buildings and collapsed the shopfront of a fashion store. Vidas was struck by flying glass and she went down, folded over at the waist and writhing in agony.

Armstrong threw himself over the journalist's crumpled body to shield her from falling debris, then scooped her limp form up into his arms. He saw Kennedy laying prone in the middle of the road, the camera discarded, the man's face awash with blood. He pointed to the injured man and the two aides dashed to his side. "Help him!"

A casualty collection point had been set up in the administration office at the train station. Armstrong carried the CMM journalist in his arms. He kicked in the door and laid her prone form on the closest table. The room was filled with a handful of paratrooper medics waiting morbidly for the day's procession of injured and dead to arrive. One of them examined the journalist, peeling off her flak-jacket and then tearing hastily at her blood-soaked shirt.

"She's got some glass fragments," the medic made a cursory inspection. "Her shoulder's not too bad..." he probed the wound with his finger, "...and she has another laceration on her hip." He turned and shouted. "I need help here!"

Armstrong stepped back. His sleeve and arm were dripping wet with the woman's blood. "Will she survive?" he asked.

"Yeah," the medic said and shoved the Colonel out of the way to reach for a stainless-steel tray of surgical instruments.

"Good," Armstrong growled. "I want to kill the bitch myself as soon as she recovers."

Chapter 5:

"Go!" Colonel Stanyuta gave the order over the radio net, barking the command to his tank and APC commanders. "Attack now before the enemy can fortify their positions. Seize the bridges!"

The last of the BM-21A BelGrad launchers unleashed their missiles and under the umbrella of that unholy thunder the first Belarusian T-72 tanks advanced. Following in the tracks of the MBTs went a Battalion of dismounted infantry. The soldiers swarmed forward, clearing out houses and office buildings on the northern bank of the river, the troops alert and on edge.

The focus of the initial assault was the most westerly crossing point. The American howitzers opened fire on the approaching enemy tide, acting on grid coordinates fed from an OP in the roof of a carpet store.

The crews of 'Chaos' Battery manned their weapons with slavish devotion and practiced skill. The first rounds crashed down on the Belarusian infantry while they were still hemmed in by the narrow streets, causing catastrophic slaughter. Apartment blocks and shopfronts collapsed in upon themselves, and shrapnel flailed like bullets. The air trapped between the buildings became furnace-like as the rounds from the American howitzers rained down, turning the road to the bridge into an infernal cauldron of death and destruction. A Belarusian Lieutenant was consumed by the fireball of an explosion and vaporized. A squad of infantry died when a round collapsed the apartment building they had been ordered to clear. The hammering thunder of exploding rounds forced some men to cower in ditches and caused others to scatter, terrified.

From out of that few square yards of hell the first Belarusian tanks emerged, trundling past the outlying buildings on the northern side of the river and bulldozing forward into a tree-studded field strung with overhead high-tension wires. Four hundred meters ahead lay the Krzna and the western river crossing.

It was the moment the American paratroopers and Abrams tanks had been waiting for.

The two Abrams defending the western crossing were hull down several hundred yards south of the crossing, positioned on opposite sides of the road. A Company of paratroopers were in deep trenches close to the riverbank and in buildings by the water's edge. The moment the first Belarusian T-72s came charging through the crucible of flames and emerged into the open, a storm of gunfire was unleashed.

The two Abrams fired simultaneously. Twin forty-foot muzzle blasts ripped through the smoke-filled gloom and the pair of 120mm guns cracked back in savage recoil. A split-second later and a thousand yards down range, the rounds struck their targets. The first T-72 was hit flush on the hull. The M829A4 depleted-uranium sabot penetrator tore through the Belarusian tank's protective armor and shattered into a hail of lethal fragments, killing the three-man crew instantly in a searing flash of flames and roiling smoke. The second enemy tank was hit just as it pivoted onto the shoulder of the road. The sabot round ripped through the Belarusian tank's right side road wheels and then blew through the engine, disabling the steel beast. The hatches were thrown open and the crew bailed out of the smoldering wreck, clambering down into a battlefield thick with gunfire.

The destroyed carcasses of the lead tanks caused pandemonium in the streets north of the crossing where a Company of Belarusian T-72s were backed up ready to advance. The vehicles at the head of the column shunted the two burning tank wrecks aside, but in doing so exposed themselves to the lethal fire of the Abrams. Three more T-72s were destroyed before the road was cleared of wreckage and the surviving Belarusian MBTs were able to surge ahead.

The Belarusian infantry were having an equally difficult time advancing. Despite HMG covering fire from teams in buildings that overlooked the river, the infantry were forced to dash forward across flat open fields, straight into the teeth of a brewing storm.

The paratroopers defending the banks of the river were heavily outnumbered but well prepared. The Belarusians advanced under a pall of white smoke to conceal their charge. The Americans opened fire and the hail of bullets plucked and tugged at the drifting bank of haze. The first Belarusian soldiers began to fall. They died in ones and twos – thrown back by the impact of the bullet strikes and screaming in agony. Some Belarusians, seeing their comrades cut down in the fury, went to ground in the long grass and blazed terrified gunfire at the far bank of the river. Others continued to move forward cautiously. Only the brave ran headlong into the cauldron of death.

A burly Belarusian Sergeant waved his arm and beckoned his men to follow him. He had been hit in the shoulder but refused to surrender to the pain of the wound. He roared at the men about him, his voice huge and desperate, urging them to keep advancing through the long grass. *"Napierad!"* he shouted himself hoarse. "Forward!"

Only a handful of the nearby soldiers responded. They followed the Sergeant through the drifting smoke, crouched low and firing blindly. As the Sergeant dashed forward, rifle fire cracked all around him. He saw bodies in the long grass. Some were dead, their corpses already swarming with flies. Others lay groaning, clutching at gruesome bloody wounds. They sobbed in pitiful agony and whimpered for help.

"Follow me!" the Sergeant bellowed to give himself courage. "Follow me!"

But most of the Belarusians within earshot had stubbornly refused to move. Instead, they dropped lumpen and doughy-faced to the ground and opened fire without clear targets. Some of the cowering troops edged backwards, wild-eyed with terror.

The Sergeant ran on, then suddenly slowed in his heroic charge and turned to see just a couple of men running at his shoulder. The rest were nowhere to be seen, lost in the swirling haze. He stopped ignominiously, and turned back, sobbing tears of humiliation and bitter outrage. *"Bajazliucy!"* he howled. "Cowards!"

An American bullet fired from the far side of the river hit the Belarusian Sergeant in the back of the head, tearing a fist-sized chunk of shattered bone and bloody gore out through the front of his skull. His head jerked then flopped to the side as his lifeless corpse dropped to the ground like a felled tree. It was the instant that broke the momentum of the Belarusian infantry assault and transformed the raw soldiers into a mob teetering on the edge of collapse.

"Fall back!" a voice in the smoke sounded thick with panic. "Retreat! Retreat!" The cry was taken up and repeated all along the ragged line.

In a single moment the wave of men spread out across the open field transformed into a panic-stricken horde. They turned and ran, terror driving them back. Some men threw down their weapons and fled sobbing with fear. Others went shuffling backwards, still firing into the distance as they withdrew.

It was over. The first Belarusian attack had failed dismally, leaving the field between the riverbank and the outskirts of the city thick with drifting smoke above a scatter of broken bodies and mangled tanks.

"Fucking spineless vermin!" Colonel Stanyuta watched the live feed from the drones circling the battlefield with a thunderous scowl. The infantry assault had been broken before it had begun, and the head of his armored column had been smashed by the American Abrams. Stanyuta raged about the command post, his fists bunched and his thoughts a murderous whirl. "This is what happens when you fight with fucking raw recruits who have never seen battle before!" he singled out his intelligence officer and flailed the man with a tirade of abuse. "A fucking disaster! A fucking humiliating screw-up, Gromyko."

The tideline of dead bodies in the grass showed the meekness of the infantry assault. The Belarusians had barely advanced a hundred yards before being repulsed and retreating. Colonel Stanyuta thrust a finger at the video screen and raged. "How can I win a war with this useless rabble?"

Major Gromyko cringed away from the Colonel. Stanyuta's expression turned savage. "We're going to attack again," he roared, "And this time the first cowardly bastard who retreats will be shot between the eyes."

The first assault had been an unmitigated disaster. Colonel Stanyuta knew that merely repeating the same tactical errors would lead to the same results. So, this time mechanized infantry aboard the BMP-2s would be carried to the riverbank before dismounting to engage the enemy. Once the Allied infantry had been overwhelmed, the ground troops would swarm across the bridgehead and hold it until the T-72s raced forward to secure the crossing.

It took a frustrating hour to clear the choked roads through the city and move the columns of armored personnel carriers forward for the attack. The BMPs emerged through a wall of white smoke, strung out in a long, ragged line between the roads leading to the western and central bridges.

Some of the BMP-2s appeared from behind groves of trees, others emerged at the end of narrow streets and surged forward. A vast patch of small farm sheds and ploughed fields was churned to muddy ruin by a wave of the trundling steel beasts. They jounced across the stretch of open field at high speed, laying down a withering wall of machine gun fire to suppress the soldiers on the far bank of the river.

To support the attack, Belarusian mortar fire pounded the Allied positions, adding to the clamor and chaos. The mortars were old Soviet 120mm 2S12 'Sani' units that had been towed to the site by trucks and were served by five-man crews. The first HE rounds landed well south of the riverbank, exploding amongst abandoned houses and setting several buildings on fire. The smoke rolled across the battlefield as the officers commanding each heavy mortar quickly adjusted their ranges. The second salvo landed directly amongst the trenches on the far bank.

With the weapons zeroed in, the barrage quickly reached a fury as the mortar crews poured a torrent of metal down on the river's edge. The explosions churned the ground and quivered the air with the shriek of each inbound shell. The paratroopers hunched down in their mud-filled trenches as the ground around them was heaved apart. One mortar round exploded killing two paratroopers in a thunder of blood and fire. Another round streaked through the smoke-stained sky and exploded in the middle of the road tearing chunks from the blacktop and stripping nearby trees of their foliage. The sound of each fresh explosion rumbled like thunder.

The American paratroopers endured the bombardment with stoic resolve. Between each huge heaving explosion they could hear the bellow of approaching engines. The air stank of fresh blood and diesel fumes as the ground beneath them trembled.

The two Abrams tanks defending the western crossing attempted to stem the advance of the enemy BMP-2s but they had a limited field of fire forward from their positions by the roadside, and so the task of thwarting the Belarusian steel tide was left to the Javelin teams, firing from trenches and from building windows. Four enemy troop carriers were destroyed by streaking Javelin missiles but the paratroopers knew that not all the weapon reloads in the world could stop the horde of BMPs before they reached the riverbank.

Karl Armstrong returned to his command post in time to see the wave of BMP-2s break from the cover of the far buildings and dash forward, popping smoke grenades to conceal their advance. He stared through the window, grim-faced. As he watched, a Javelin team launched a missile in 'Direct Attack' mode. The weapon streaked across the river on a fiery tail of smoke and plunged down into the hull of a BMP, blowing the vehicle into a smoking flaming tangle of twisted metal and killing everyone aboard. "They're trying to push us back to clear the way for their armor," the American Colonel understood the enemy's plan immediately, yet wondered if that knowledge helped at all. His men were heavily outnumbered and outgunned. All they had was their stubbornness and their skill.

Charlie Mott came swarming up the stairs. He was in command of the troops defending the central river crossing where, so far, there had been little enemy activity. He flinched instinctively as an enemy mortar shell landed close by the building, then seized Armstrong's arm. His hand came away bloody.

"Are you injured?"

Armstrong shook his head. "That damned woman journalist got hit by some glass fragments. I carried her to the aid station."

Mott grunted, and perhaps would have said more if the news he carried had not been so important. "We just got word from NATO," he said in a rush between enemy mortar explosions. "Help is on its way. Command is flying in the rest of the 173rd Airborne Brigade from Vincenza to reinforce us."

Armstrong blinked, torn for an instant between relief and concern. The Sky Soldiers were not the best-equipped Allied troops to handle an enemy mechanized brigade bristling with T-72 MBTs. "How soon?"

"That's the bad news," Mott shrugged. "HQ wants us to hold up the enemy invasion force for eighteen hours. The earliest we can expect to see chutes in the sky is midday tomorrow."

Armstrong swore, then nodded with a soldier's fatalistic acceptance of things beyond his control. He turned his attention back to the unfolding battle. The ragged line of enemy BMPs were approaching the northern riverbank. Any moment now, he knew, hundreds of enemy soldiers were going to spill out through the rear doors of those steel monsters and open fire on his beleaguered troops desperately clinging to the southern bank.

Eighteen hours… Armstrong worried. *The battle for the bridges across the Krzna could be lost in the next eighteen minutes.*

*

The Belarusian line of BMP-2s braked to a halt fifty yards from the riverbank, their coaxial machine guns relentlessly hammering the air above the American trenches. From time to time the thunder of machine gun fire was overlaid by the deeper bass sound of 30mm autocannon fire, blazing away in short bursts.

As soon as the vehicles stopped, the rear doors were flung open and Belarusian mechanized infantry poured out into the long grass.

The soldiers formed up in the shelter of their vehicles and then, on command, dashed forward towards the river, firing from the hip as they closed on the American trenches. Their mission was to pin the enemy troops down while a fresh assault was mounted on the western crossing. The BMPs stopped firing as their soldiers advanced and a sudden eerie lull fell over the battlefield. It was not a silence; the Belarusian infantry were spraying the far bank with light arms fire – but after the hammering thunder of the coaxial machine guns, the battlefield sounded almost peaceful.

As soon as the infantry began their advance, a dozen more BMP-2s carrying a Company of troops emerged from the northern outskirts of the city and dashed forward along the road, driving at full speed for the crossing.

The two Abrams defending the bridge opened fire. The range was less than a thousand yards. The lead BMP-2 exploded from a direct hit but the rest of the column came on with grim determination. One of the Belarusian infantry fighting vehicles swerved to the shoulder of the blacktop, braked to a lurching halt, and fired an AT-4 'Spigot' SACLOS (semiautomatic command-to-line-of-sight) anti-tank guided missile. The weapon flew from its turret-mounted launch-tube and went whistling low over the ground on a feather of grey exhaust smoke, weaving and dipping towards the closest hull-down Abrams. The 'Spigot' struck the front turret of the Abrams and exploded, but the HEAT warhead failed to penetrate the tank's thick armor. The Abrams emerged scorched black and on fire from splashed propellant, but otherwise undamaged. The Sergeant commanding the tank took the turret hit to his Abrams as a personal affront.

"Designate APC!" he sighted the Belarusian BMP-2 through his CITV (Commander's Independent Thermal Viewer) and barked the order.

"AMP up!" the tank's loader said to alert the gunner there was already an Advance Multi-purpose round loaded into the breech.

"Identified!" the gunner's hands were trembling with adrenaline rush, then his training took over and his actions became automatic. He lased the target as he simultaneously centered the sight reticle, guiding the GPCH (Gunner's Power Control Handle) in front of him with his left hand. The handle had two triggers, two power control activation levers and two laser buttons to allow for left-or-right-hand use. He triggered the power levers and peered through the GPS, (Gunner's Primary Sight) toggling the handles until the reticle was set on the center mass of the enemy tank. The ballistic computer aboard the Abrams made adjustments for the range, wind and temperature in a nano-second. The entire process took just two hammering heartbeats.

"Fire and adjust!" the Sergeant gave the command.

The gunner crushed the trigger. "On the way!"

The Abrams rocked on its suspension as the round left the barrel at the end of a fiery dragon's breath of muzzle blast.

The projectile struck the BMP-2 front on, tearing right through the hull and exploding, blowing the vehicle apart. Fire and smoke poured from the twisted wreckage, for a moment blotting out the rest of the enemy column of vehicles.

"Target!" the gunner declared with savage triumph.

But behind the billowing pall of smoke the other BMP-2s raced bravely on, carrying their cargo of infantry towards the vital crossing. The comms unit in the American tank commander's headset sparked to life.

"Blue Two, Command. Close and engage enemy PCs!" Karl Armstrong had seen the looming threat and knew there was only one countermeasure.

The Abrams reversed from its hull-down position and came forward, still trailing tongues of licking flame and slathered in a thick coat of dust and debris. The Sergeant commanding Blue Two searched the drifting smoke for targets, acutely aware that he was driving into danger.

A tank's natural enemy is an urban warfare environment. As a rule, tanks prefer vast open spaces where they are free to maneuver and engage the enemy from longer range. Being hemmed in by narrow streets and tall buildings made tankers nervous because they were so vulnerable to MANPATS (man-portable anti-tank systems). Now, as the Abrams emerged from its entrenched position, the crew in the belly of the steel beast became acutely aware of the risk they were taking.

The Abrams charged forward, firing on the move as the distance between the vehicle and the approaching BMP-2s closed. Three more Belarusian APCs were destroyed in quick succession, turning the road on the north side of the bridge into a charnel house of twisted burning debris. Scorched and blackened bodies lay amidst the wreckage. Severed limbs and gore were strewn across the blacktop. The remaining BMP commanders lost their nerve and braked to a halt on the shoulder of the road, still two hundred yards short of the crossing. They slewed around in the gravel and the rear doors of the troop carriers burst open. Men spilled out into the thick smoking cauldron and came sprinting forward in a suicidal effort to seize the crossing.

"Gunner! Coax troops!" the Sergeant commanding Blue Two saw the enemy infantry through the flames and drifting haze.

The Sergeant manned the tank's CROWS system (Common Remotely Operated Weapons Station) and opened fire on the Belarusian infantry with the Abrams' 50cal from within the turret while the tank's gunner operated the coax.

Between the two flame-spitting machine guns, they took a terrible toll.

It was savage slaughter. The enemy infantry were caught on the blacktop and decimated. The heavy 50cal machine gun mounted atop the Abrams tore the attack to pieces, dismembering bodies and turning flesh to pulp. Guts and gore were sprayed across the blacktop and still the heavy machine gun hammered the air until the road ahead was empty and the attack destroyed.

The Abrams continued to trundle forward. It reached the bridge, grinding dead enemy bodies beneath its churning steel tracks as it closed on the parked BMP-2s. The blacktop looked like a slaughter yard. Belarusian soldiers lay in twisted attitudes of agony, their chests ripped open, the gaping wounds swarming with flies. They were piled in clumps around the northern side of the crossing, the gravel verge stained dark brown with blood. The Belarusian vehicle commanders gunned their engines and scattered for their lives like sheep with a wolf in their midst. The Abrams continued to fire, the tank's crew slavishly serving the barking 120mm gun. Two more BMP-2s were destroyed before they could retreat to safety.

"Blue Two, fall back," Karl Armstrong had watched the battle for the bridge and seen the unholy chaos the single Abrams had wrecked upon the enemy. The tank began to reverse and then a streak of white light on a wavering tail of smoke flashed towards the vehicle. The RPG had been fired from the riverbank where the Belarusian infantry were engaged in a fierce close-range firefight with the American paratroopers on the far side of the river.

"RPG!" the tank's driver saw the approaching missile and had just a split-second to raise the alarm.

The RPG (rocket propelled grenade) was a remarkably simple weapon, easy to fire and highly reliable. It was operated by a two-man crew; the assistant preparing the projectile and the gunner loading, then shouldering the weapon to fire. It first saw action in the 1967 Arab-Israeli War and has been in operation with armies and insurgent groups around the world ever since.

The projectile struck the Abrams tank's right-side and the steel beast disappeared behind a flash of flame and a swirling grey cloud of smoke. The wicked '*crack!*' of the explosion echoed across the battlefield. When the haze cleared the Abrams two rear roadwheels and the raised driving sprocket were buckled and blackened, rendering the sixty-ton monster disabled.

Karl Armstrong swore, and swore again. He could see the tank slewed across the road, the steel track cast off its idler wheel and return rollers. He could see, too, that the enemy infantry on the far side of the riverbank were preparing to fire a second projectile at the hapless Abrams. Over the shouting and screams and the ceaseless chatter of light arms fire from along the banks of the river he heard the tank's 50cal machine gun suddenly roar back into life.

From inside the turret of the Abrams the Sergeant re-took control of the CROWS system and peered through the thermal camera as he thumbed the joystick, bringing the 50cal to bear on the Belarusian infantry along the riverbank. The heavy machine gun opened fire, churning the air with its roaring thunder. Two BMP-2s parked close together were disabled by multiple armor-penetrating hits that killed the drivers and commanders in both vehicles and hacked the men in the grass nearby to pieces. But the two-man crew operating the RPG-7 held their nerve just long enough to fire off a second projectile before the ground around them was churned to dust by a flail of bullets.

The high explosive anti-tank warhead struck the Abrams broadside, detonating, but failing to penetrate the vehicle's armor. The blast shook the tank, rattling the crew inside the hull. The hatches were thrown open and the four men bailed out of the stricken vehicle. Enemy machine gun fire slashed and zipped at their heels as they dashed into the long grass seeking cover.

The loss of the Abrams was a cruel blow to the Americans, but the Belarusians too were suffering terribly along the riverbank. Almost a quarter of the troop carriers that had launched the attack were now disabled or destroyed, their smoldering wrecks adding to the dense pall of smoke that sifted across the riverbank. Some of the vehicles began to edge back from the river, firing off smoke grenades to conceal their positions, whilst in the grass around them the infantry still doggedly fought on.

The paratroopers in their trenches bravely began to return fire, picking off enemy infantry targets and adding to the rising Belarusian death toll. The combatants were so close they were throwing grenades across the river at each other, the *'crump!'* of the explosions churning the earth into a turmoil of mud and blood. A paratrooper Sergeant saw three enemy infantry in the grass, sheltering in the lee of a BMP and opened fire, killing one of the men and injuring another. The wounded man flopped on the ground, thrashing and screaming in pain. The unscathed soldier in the group shouldered his weapon and dragged his bleeding comrade away from the riverbank, using the maimed man as an excuse to flee the fighting. Close by, two more Belarusians were in the long grass, cut down by an American grenade. One man's face was a bloody mask from a head wound and the other was on his hands and knees, clutching at a gaping hole in his guts. He heaved in short tight breaths, overcome with the agony of his wounds, pleading desperately for help.

The Sky Soldiers too suffered casualties. A dozen men were wounded and a handful more were dead, most killed by enemy grenades. They lay unmoving at the bottom of their trenches, their blood soaking the earth, while the men around them stumbled and staggered over their limp bodies to continue the frantic fight. One paratrooper wrenched himself away from a spray of gunfire at the exact instant an enemy soldier aimed and squeezed his trigger. A bullet creased the paratrooper's helmet and deflected away into the haze. The American returned fire and missed, then was shot in the neck and thrown down into the mud, screaming in shock, blood spilling through his fingers as his body began convulsing.

Colonel Stanyuta watched the lone American Abrams tank tear the heart out of his attempt to seize the bridge with impotent rage. Hunched in front of the monitor displaying the drone feed, he sat aghast, livid red spots of frustration coloring his unshaven cheeks. He saw the dead infantry sprawled and slaughtered across the road and the black tangled carnage of half-a-dozen destroyed BMP-2s, some still burning fiercely.

He flicked his focus to the infantry battle along the riverfront and realized it was now utterly pointless. "Call off the attack," he turned to one of his aides. "Give the order immediately. Get the infantry and APCs out of there before we lose the lot of them for no gain."

The aide scurried away to give the orders leaving Stanyuta alone with his bitter frustration. He had a full mechanized brigade of tanks and troops, but due to the nature of the Allied defenses and the tight confines of the city they were fighting in, only a small portion of his force could be brought to battle, negating the one advantage he had; a massive numerical and materiel superiority. He bounced to his feet and began to pace the ground in front of his command vehicle, his hands clenched tight behind his back and his head bowed. Soviet military doctrine, in which he had been so thoroughly trained, had always relied on a weight of numbers behind a massed artillery barrage to win the day. But that only applied in situations where a numerical advantage could be exploited…

He wrestled with the problem for several minutes and then suddenly froze as an idea pressed in on him. The notion came ghosting along his spine and then bloomed bright and obvious in his imagination.

Outflank the bastards!

He turned on his heel and called urgently for maps. Suddenly his heart was pounding in his chest and in his eyes was a cunning spark of savage malice.

An aide arrived clutching a map of the frontier. Stanyuta unrolled the chart and studied it quickly, searching… searching…

"There!" he exclaimed and stabbed the map with his thumb. Six kilometers south east of the city were more bridges. He turned and bellowed for his operations officer.

"Send a Battalion of T-72s and two Battalions of Mechanized infantry to encircle the enemy positions," he pointed to the map and described the encircling motion with an expressive hand gesture. "Divert the closest units off the highway and send them cross country. And I want artillery support," he snapped as an afterthought. His heavy guns were still miles back down the road. Now, rather than bring them to the battlefront he would haul them off the highway to support a second attack behind the enemy's right flank. "We are being held up by just a couple of hundred paratroopers and maybe some Polish regulars who are all lined along the riverbank," he said forcefully. "Their flank will be completely undefended. If we move quickly, we can seize the airfield and train station before they realize we have kicked in their back door while they weren't looking."

Colonel Stanyuta beamed with wolfish anticipation and then checked himself. To guarantee success he needed one more thing; a diversion – which meant more men would have to die.

Chapter 6:

The Belarusian infantry and the surviving BMP-2s withdrew from the riverbank, hounded by American howitzer fire as they retreated. In the aftermath, the battlefield was consumed by an eerie, uneasy silence. The paratroopers emerged from their trenches, dazed and exhausted. The smoke-sifted fields had been churned to mud, the ground strewn with dead and dying. On the far side of the blood-soaked riverbank, Belarusian soldiers could be heard, some groaning in agony, others sobbing with the pain of their wounds and pleading desperately for help.

The American paratroopers climbed from their trenches and sat in the grass like the survivors of some dreadful natural disaster. Their eyes were vacant, their faces drawn, and their movements mechanical as they gulped down water, lit cigarettes and reloaded their weapons. Smoke drifted across the riverbank from the burning ruins of the BMP-2s, draping a grey blanket over the scene of gruesome slaughter.

Medics moved amongst the Sky Soldiers, tending to light wounds with bandages and stretchering the seriously injured and dead to waiting Humvees for transport to the casualty collection point at the train station.

At his command post, Karl Armstrong slumped against a window sill and watched a Humvee speed away carrying three wounded men. His mind was a whirl of regrets and relief so that it was several long moments before he realized he was not alone. He turned, frowning, and saw the slim figure of Janna Vidas standing in the open doorway.

The journalist had changed her shirt. She had thick gauze padding on her shoulder and the shape of more bandages strapped at her hip, just above the waistband of her denim jeans. She stared across the small room and her gaze was solemn and enigmatic. "I'm sorry for the interruption," her tone sounded contrite. "Major Mott said I would find you here."

Armstrong said nothing. Janna Vidas made a flustered placating gesture with her hands. "I… I wanted to thank you," she took a single step into the room, wary and uncertain. "My cameraman told me you saved my life."

"I'm relieved you're okay," Armstrong was aware of the unintended harshness in his voice and regretted it. "I'm glad your injuries weren't more serious."

She took another step, then began drifting around the room as though wrestling for a way to bridge the brittle chasm between them. She moved with the easy grace of a dancer, her delicate fingers fluttering at her side.

"I owe you a great debt of gratitude," she said softly, "but I won't apologize, Colonel. I know you think I was acting recklessly. I wasn't. I was doing my job."

"Your job?" Armstrong felt the hairs on the back of his neck bristle. "What exactly is your job, Miss Vidas?" his tone hardened.

"Reporting on this monstrous war," she shot back. Her body stiffened and her hands bunched. Her expression darkened and turned truculent. "Someone needs to tell the plight of the innocent Belarusians. Everyone in America thinks the Belarusians and Russians are part of evil an empire. They're not!" her voice rose an octave and a flush of hostile color bloomed on her cheeks. "Belarusians are a peace-loving people ruled by a despot and manipulated by a dictator in Moscow. That's the story I'm here to tell."

"Peace-loving?" Armstrong bridled. "The Belarusian Army just surged across the Bug River into Poland killing everything in sight."

"They have been manipulated!" Vidas shot back defensively. "I know Belarus, Colonel. My mother was born in Minsk and my father is from Vladivostok in Russia. I grew up in this part of the world. It's quite possible the Belarusian troops were provoked into an attack by the belligerence of the Polish Army along the border."

Armstrong gaped. He glared at the journalist, incredulity twisting his features to stone. "You think this damned war we're fighting is some kind of accident?"

"I think the Polish Government is playing the Americans and the Allies for fools," she retorted. "What's happening right now is a misunderstanding, and nothing more. Belarus and Russia do not want war. Their hands have been forced by NATO denying peace in the Baltics."

"A misunderstanding…?" Karl Armstrong seized on the word and his face contorted into an ugly spasm of hatred. "A misunderstanding?"

Without another word his hand lashed out and clamped like a vice around Janna Vidas' arm, wrenching her off balance. He dragged her down the stairs. She went, twisting and shouting at him, as he dragged her ignominiously into the street. A Humvee carrying the bodies of two dead paratroopers was edging away from the muddy riverbank. Armstrong stepped out into the middle of the road and the vehicle lurched to a sudden stop. Armstrong dragged the struggling journalist to the rear tray of the vehicle and shoved her cruelly.

"Take a look," he barked, seething. "There's your fucking story! These brave patriots made the ultimate sacrifice. They were fighting for freedom and they laid down their lives. They were killed by Belarusian machine guns."

One dead man's face was a ruin of mangled flesh and gore. Both his eyes had been torn out by grenade fragments. The top of his head was swathed in blood and mud-soaked bandages and the expression frozen on his lifeless distorted features was a rictus of agony. He had died hard, in slow, cruel pain. The other corpse was that of a pale-faced young man, his features in death eerily soft and serene. He had been shot twice in the groin and had bled out before the gaping wounds could be staunched.

"You call this a misunderstanding?" Armstrong's voice was savage. "There's no fucking misunderstanding here, lady! The Belarusians and the Russians *are* evil. They're warmongers wreaking ruin and havoc across Europe for their own political gain. Film this! Film the real horror of war!" He let go of her arm and she twisted away from him, her hair tangled in disarray across her face, her breathing coming in sharp horrified gasps and her eyes wide with revulsion. She lost her balance and instinctively threw out a hand to steady herself. Her fingers brushed one of the dead corpses. The flesh was cold. She cringed away, then sank to the ground. Her body shook with huge heaving sobs, the sound of each one like something deep inside her was tearing.

*

The tank crew removed the remaining main gun ammunition from the hull of the disabled Abrams and distributed the rounds amongst the surviving seven tanks. Then the small arms, the crew-served ammunition, and all the crew-served weapons, including the heavy 50cal machine gun, were offloaded before the steel monster was scuttled with a handful of thermite grenades. The paratroopers who had so stoically defended the western crossing re-dug their trenches while boiling black smoke from the burning tank spread across the afternoon sky.

The southern bank of the river was scoured a final time for dead bodies, as men took a long poignant moment to remember their fallen comrades, huddling together in solemn groups to pay their respects.

The paratroopers defending the center bridge helped repair the trench line while engineers filled sandbags to fortify each emplacement. Ammunition taken from the weapons of the dead and injured was shared amongst the survivors as they worked on, ever wary that at any moment a fresh Belarusian attack could come pouring out of the northern outskirts of the city.

Karl Armstrong walked amongst the Sky Soldiers as they dug, stopping to chat quietly with his men. The soldiers worked stripped to their waists, downcast but determined. A pall of quiet despair hung over the riverbank. Every paratrooper had lost a close friend in the fighting, and every man was mourning in their own way.

A Corporal carried a tin mug of steaming coffee across the crater-strewn ground and handed it to the Colonel. "Thought you might like a drink, sir," the man said. His eyes were red and his face was streaked with sweat and caked with dust. Armstrong accepted the mug and nodded his thanks. The Corporal offered Armstrong a cigarette and then cupped his hand around the flame of a lighter. The two men stared, smoking silently, across the carnage of the battlefield like old friends, rank set aside, bonded in their grief.

"If they come again," the Corporal drew deeply on his cigarette and filled his lungs, "I reckon I'll be the first one killed," he said with bleak fatalism.

Colonel Armstrong blinked. "What makes you say that, son?"

The Corporal shrugged. "It's my time," he said. "I should have died during the first attack. Steve Mills took a bullet for me," his voice wavered suddenly as his composure cracked and his terror came flooding to the surface. "We were in a trench by the river," his bottom lip trembled. "I'd emptied my mag into a group of enemy soldiers and as I was reloading, one of the fuckers returned fire. Stevie threw himself in front of me – took two rounds in the head. He… he was dead before I could catch his falling body." The words trailed off into a series of sobbing breaths. Armstrong looked down and saw the Corporal's hands were caked in dry blood, and there were more spattered stains on his uniform shirt.

The Colonel said nothing. The young Corporal's shoulders began to heave and the gasp of anguish he had been choking on was suddenly torn from his lips. Armstrong stared hard into the young soldier's face. There was nothing he could say to console the man; words were wholly inadequate and the Colonel had seen enough of war's horror to know that.

"I want you to report to the Casualty Collection Station," Armstrong said, his voice gentling. "I need to be sure we've collected all the spare ammunition and that it's been distributed to men who can use it. Can you do that for me, soldier?"

The Corporal nodded, cuffed irritably at his tears, suddenly embarrassed, and trudged towards the road, his feet leaden and his shoulders hunched as if guilt was crushing the life out of him. Armstrong watched the man until he disappeared behind a speeding Humvee.

Charlie Mott climbed down from the vehicle and strode to the riverbank. His face was dark with worry.

"Nine dead and fourteen wounded," the Major gave Armstrong the casualty count. "The medics think a couple of the injured won't make it to sunset…"

Armstrong winced. Victory had come at a heavy price.

"We've also got an injured CMM cameraman and female journalist who says you assaulted her," Charlie Mott sounded deeply uncomfortable delivering the news. "She's threatening to take her complaint to Headquarters."

"Let her," Armstrong said vehemently.

Charlie Mott gave a wan little smile as though he had expected the retort. "Fine by me," he shrugged. "But if you ever want that full bird…"

"Aw shit, Charlie!" Armstrong seethed. "The bitch is a propaganda poster for the fuckin' Russians in a bra and tight jeans. She's interested in one thing only; broadcasting her anti-American, anti-war message to anyone naïve enough to listen to her."

"Maybe," Mott conceded, ever the diplomat. He kept his voice reasonable as he went on, delicately choosing his words. "But she's also an accredited journalist, and she has HQ's permission to be here. And until you make the effort to mend bridges, she's going to be an enemy we haven't got the time or resources to fight. There's a war going on right in front of us."

"You want me to apologize to the commie bitch?" Armstrong's tone turned truculent, though he secretly suspected Mott's diplomatic solution was the only sensible way forward.

"Yes."

*

The Belarusian command staff officers were all assembled and waiting when Colonel Stanyuta emerged from the gloom of his BTR-80AK and announced his revised plans.

"Our objectives remain the same. All that matters is capturing the airfield and the train station. But since we cannot force our way across the bridges the Allies hold, we are going to outsmart the bastards. I have given orders for tanks and APCs supported by heavy artillery to sweep around to the east of the city and overrun the enemy's positions," he announced, then turned to his operations officer. "How long before the outflanking force will be ready to attack?"

"Perhaps another hour, no more than two." The Battalion of T-72s needed to be re-routed off the highway as did the APCs carrying the mechanized infantry units. It was no small task.

Stanyuta grumbled. He glowered at the harried officer. "If it takes any longer, I'll have your balls."

The operations officer nodded with a jerk of his head, and the Colonel searched the assembled faces for an artillery Major. "Kisly, your howitzers will be ready when we need them, yes? You know what is required?"

"Certainly, Colonel," the man answered. "I have three batteries already in place to the east ready to support the attack."

"Good," Stanyuta allowed himself the barest flicker of a smile, then moved on to the real reason for this briefing. "In order to ensure surprise, we are going to attack the bridges again. The eastern one this time, I think," he mulled the question over for a moment, then decided. "Yes, the eastern one. The attack will be merely a diversion to keep the enemy from looking over their shoulder, so I don't want to waste good men on the assault. I need some cannon fodder; troops who are expendable. Suggestions?"

"We have two Battalions of raw recruits fresh from the Minsk depots," an infantry Major offered. He was a gruff, ill-tempered pig of a man with a rasping voice coarsened by forty years of chain-smoking cigarettes.

Stanyuta considered the option and finally nodded. "Good. We'll send one Battalion forward after a salvo of rocket and mortar fire. That should be enough to keep the Americans occupied. But hold the other Battalion nearby in reserve, just in case they are needed."

The sun disappeared behind a bank of drifting black smoke and the afternoon turned suddenly chill as the Belarusians finalized their plans. A Battalion of raw infantry would advance on the eastern bridge after a brief rocket barrage while, six kilometers to the south east, a Battalion of T-72 tanks supported by two Battalions of Mechanized Infantry encircled the enemy and launched the real attack under the umbrella of heavy howitzer fire.

Satisfied, Stanyuta glanced at his wristwatch. It was almost one o'clock in the afternoon. By four o'clock the killing should be done, and the airstrip and train station seized. Then he could continue his push west towards Warsaw. He called to an aide for a bottle of vodka and raised his glass. "To dead Americans and to victory in Poland."

The officers dutifully repeated the toast, and upended their glasses.

*

The woman on the street corner was impatient and clearly terrified. Janna Vidas had her cornered against a brick wall while her cameraman, 'Tosh' Kennedy, his forehead swathed in fresh bandages, prepared to film.

"You speak English, yes?" Vidas questioned the woman.

"Yes," she nodded. She was an English teacher and a Belarusian native who had moved to Poland because well-paying teaching jobs were more plentiful. She had remained in her home when the city had been evacuated, and now the rockets and mortars and tanks and gunfire had left her deeply regretting her stubborn decision.

"This will only take a minute," Vidas calmed the woman with a reassuring smile. "The people in America want to hear how you feel about the fighting taking place right now around Biala Podlaska."

The woman cast a nervous glance down the length of the road and seeing no tanks and hearing no gunfire, reluctantly agreed with a jerking nod of her head. Vidas pressed at her hair and practiced her smile, then signaled to Kennedy. "Let's do it."

The camera began recording and Vidas introduced the woman, giving a succinct explanation of her circumstances and a description of the recent battle for the western bridge, then turned and thrust her microphone under the woman's chin.

"You're a Belarusian national, living in Poland," the journalist set up the question. "How do you feel about Belarusian tanks on the streets of Biala Podlaska?"

"They had no other choice," the woman defended the invasion stoutly. "The Polish provoked this incident. I heard from my brother-in-law in Minsk last night that Polish tanks and armed soldiers had crossed the Belarusian border and slaughtered over a thousand innocent women and children in a township in western Belarus. Our Army had no choice but to drive the Poles back across the Bug River and punish them for their savage assault."

"Do you blame Poland for the current crisis developing in western Europe?"

"Of course," the woman said. "It is the work of the corrupt Polish Government," she added, warming to her cause. "And the interfering American politicians in Washington."

Karl Armstrong came striding around the corner and did a double-take when he saw the journalist standing at the intersection. Janna Vidas recognized the Colonel and her eyes flashed with savage malice. The moment Armstrong lifted his eyes to hers; she raised her chin in a gesture of contemptuous disdain, then turned her attention to the woman against the wall, listening intently to what she was saying and then repeating her comments loudly enough for Armstrong to hear.

"So, you believe the Polish Government provoked the Belarusians, and that the actions of Belarus' Army are entirely justified, right?" she summarized, her throaty voice dripping poison.

"Yes," the woman nodded.

"And do you believe American soldiers should be fighting this war?"

"No," the woman scowled. "Europeans should be free to determine their own future. The American soldiers should go home."

Vidas smiled, the expression twisted with venomous satisfaction, then thanked the woman. She turned to the camera. "This is Janna Vidas reporting from the European battlefront in Biala Podlaska, Poland, for CMM."

Kennedy lowered the camera from his shoulder and Vidas thanked the Belarusian woman again. Karl Armstrong took two stilted steps towards the journalist, tight-lipped and bitterly resenting the need to mollify the woman with an apology.

Janna Vidas watched him approach, secretly gloating, and then a high-pitched shriek filled the sky, followed a moment later by the thunderous tremor of an explosion.

Karl Armstrong turned on his heel and sprinted for the riverbank.

*

The troops given the task of advancing to the eastern bridge were the leavings of Colonel Stanyuta's Mechanized Brigade; raw recruits scraped from the bottom of the barrels at Minsk's depots and sent west to bolster the force that swept into Poland. They were armed with antiquated AK-47 assault rifles and a smattering of AKMs. They were dressed in mismatched uniforms and none wore body armor. They were transported to the staging point for the attack in trucks, crammed together like cattle on the way to the abattoir.

The three Companies of infantry dismounted and formed ranks in a shopping center parking lot. They were led by a handful of first-year Officer cadets, elevated to a level of command far beyond their experience. Most of the raw recruits were fresh faced and terrified. They could hear their artillery pounding the enemy's positions. The dreadful thunder of the rockets and the imminent approach of combat made some sob quietly.

NCOs marched between the ranks, bellowing. They were big brawny men with scarred scowling faces and huge bullying voices.

"One magazine!" they shouted. "If you're carrying more than one magazine, you are to hand it over to the nearest Sergeant when he passes you. You're not going to engage the enemy in a firefight so you won't need more than a single magazine of bullets. You're going to charge and seize the bridge, not lay in the grass wasting ammunition."

Then the barked messages took on a more sinister tone as the Sergeants singled out the weak and the trembling, their voices carrying to every corner of the parking lot.

"You will not retreat!" they roared. "If you retreat, you will be shot."

"You will keep charging until you seize the bridge. If you turn away or cower from the fight, your family will be told of your cowardice and you will be shunned for life."

"You will not retreat. If you take a single cowardly step backwards from the enemy, your loved ones at home will be punished."

"You will not stop to give aid to any of your wounded comrades. You will keep advancing to the bridge."

The litany went on until the young soldiers were cowered and cringing, even more terrified of the consequences of failure than anything the enemy's guns might soon throw at them.

The last of the rockets exploded on the far side of the river and a whistle sounded. The infantry marched in columns to the northern outskirts of the city and then formed into two long lines at the edge of a grassy meadow. Four hundred yards ahead of them, where the river and the bridge should be, was nothing but a boiling mist of black heaving smoke and licking flames.

One young soldier folded at the waist and vomited over his boots. Another man choked back a terrified moan. From somewhere else within their ranks a man began chanting feverish prayers to his God.

Another whistle sounded, this one longer and shriller. A Lieutenant in the center of the first line turned and licked dry, trembling lips.

"Advance." His voice was thin, tremulous and uncertain. He took a few tentative steps forward and the rest of the line followed him. Some men jogged, eager to get the terror over with. Most walked stiffly, their eyes huge and swimming as the meadow's long grass swished about their knees.

The men who had dashed ahead of the line quickly slowed, realizing they were making targets of themselves. On the left flank, a dozen soldiers waded out of the field's long grass and onto the road that led directly to the bridge.

The lines went forward, ragged and wavering, each man holding his breath, his heart jammed in his throat as the smoke on the far riverbank began to thin and they could see at last the bridge and burning buildings beyond. The far riverbank was a gentle mud-churned slope, cratered and torn to turmoil. Surely, the Belarusian soldiers prayed fervently, no enemy soldiers could have survived the thundering hammer blows of massed rocket artillery that had swarmed across the sky.

The infantry kept advancing, but their steps shortened. They began to bunch together as they pressed towards to the river. No one spoke. No one shouted. Their mouths turned dry; their legs trembled. They were cowered by fear and whipped on by the lash of their Sergeants who kept barking the humiliating consequences of cowardice until they were within a hundred and fifty yards of their objective.

"Now charge and cheer, you bastards!" the Sergeants broke the eerie silence. "Charge!"

Major Nowak peered forward from the shelter of a riverbank trench and saw drifting shapes in the distance, fading in and out of the swirling smoke, and then he heard a roar of strangled voices and realized an enemy attack was closing on his position. As the smoke from the rocket barrage thinned the meadow on the far side of the bridge appeared as a hazy nightmare of shell-churned ground filled with a swarm of shouting, running enemy soldiers.

"Oh, God!" He could hear the shrill bellows of the charging enemy and the sound of their pounding boots, and all he could do for several long seconds was stare, dumbfounded and utterly paralysed with bowel-churning fear. The troops in the trenches gaped at the Major, waiting for the order to open fire as the swarm of Belarusian infantry closed within a hundred yards of the river.

The Polish Major had two companies of men dug in defending the crossing and a reserve company in trucks, waiting at the airstrip two miles to the south.

"Fire!" Major Nowak blurted at last.

The Polish infantry opened fire on the mass of enemy soldiers and the range was so close and the Belarusians so densely packed together that scarcely a gun could miss. One moment the ground on the far side of the river was heaving with a dark swarm of soldiers and the next it was a charnel house, flailed and thrashed by spitting, flickering flame and yet more smoke.

Colonel Armstrong saw the enemy advance through the drifting skeins of haze and called in a Fire Mission for the howitzers. The crews of the six M777s adjusted their guns to the Target Point by entering the data into their digital fire control systems, and thirty seconds later the big guns added their own throaty roar to the chaos and clamor.

The M777 howitzers were each served by eight cannoneers working together in a choreographed routine that allowed the guns to fire up to four rounds every minute. The howitzers were loaded with M982 Excalibur rounds; a GPS-guided HE round that had fin stabilization and a programmable guidance system to ensure near pinpoint accuracy.

"Fire!"

The first salvo erupted from the barrels of the howitzers and went shrieking across the sky towards the northern bank of the river, plunging down through the smoke to land amongst the Belarusian infantry with devastating effect. Men were cut down as if cleaved by a scythe as the rounds rained down in fireballs and billowing smoke.

"Fire Mission! Fire Mission! Let's go!" the American howitzer crews raced forward to service their guns, reloading with a fresh round and a propellant charge. Two men thrust the round home with a seven-foot-long J Rammer, known to the crews as a 'Banana Rammer', and then stepped quickly back.

"Good ram! Good ram! Let's go, let's go, let's go!" the Gun Chief barked encouragement.

A long lanyard chord connected to the firing mechanism was taken up by a man standing to the right of the gun, his back turned to the barrel. The rest of the crew retreated from the massive gun's recoil.

"Hook up!" the Gun Chief roared, then, "Standby!"

There was a heartbeat of tense, heavy silence. After a dramatic pause the Gun Chief swept his arm savagely down. "Fire!"

The man holding the lanyard line twisted his upper body violently, wrenching the cord and triggering the gun. The howitzer heaved back in recoil and a billow of dust enveloped the weapon.

"Let's go! Let's go! Let's go!" the men dashed forward again.

The second salvo of rounds fell in the meadow of crushed grass and churned earth. The noise of each explosion echoed on the air, turning the field into an inferno. More enemy troops were cut down by the murderous onslaught. One Belarusian soldier clapped his hands to his face and reeled away, blood streaming through his fingers. The man beside him fell to his hands and knees, his guts sliced open by shrapnel. He vomited blood into a patch of thorns and moaned pitifully for help.

Behind the Allied lines, the cannoneers continued to slavishly serve their guns, knowing that every second was critical.

"Fire!" the Gun Chief's arm swept down again.

The cannoneers holding the lanyards heaved and wrenched their torsos again, and again the battery of howitzers barked their deadly fury. The salvo of rounds landed close to the northern edge of the riverbank but by now there were so few Belarusian infantry left standing that the salvo was largely ineffective. Explosions flared bright amidst the smoke and the thunder of each blast rolled across the sky, and when the haze drifted south, carried on the breeze, all that remained of the attack was a slaughter yard of blood-soaked grass and a ghastly litter of dismembered churned flesh, crawling with flies and steaming in the afternoon sun.

Major Nowak rose cautiously from the depths of his trench and stared, sickened, at the carnage. His senses were overwhelmed, his ears still echoing with the crashing thunder of the battle so that it was several seconds before a disturbing rumble of distant artillery fire registered dimly in his addled mind. He turned, puzzled, trying to pinpoint the direction of the sound, and saw a red-faced aide running towards him in a lather of sweat.

"Sir! The Belarusians have launched a surprise attack from the east. They're behind our flank and driving tanks and APCs directly for the airstrip."

Chapter 7:

Major Nowak received the shocking news with such astonishment that for several seconds he did nothing. The color drained from his face and he gaped, then wrenched his head to the east as if he expected to see enemy tanks burst through a grove of nearby trees. An Army Ford Ranger appeared on the street corner and Nowak knew his duty. "Take me to the airstrip," he said manfully. "Does the American Colonel know what is happening?"

"He has been informed, sir," the aide assured the Major.

The driver drove like he was possessed by demons and the Ranger sped along the narrow roads, swerving around fallen rubble and cratered sections of blacktop. Nowak's reserve Company of Polish soldiers were assembled on the eastern edge of the airstrip, the Captain commanding the troops barking frantic orders for his men to find cover.

But there was scant shelter to be had. The ground east of the runway consisted of miles of undulating farm fields, sprinkled with groves of trees and cut through by small bubbling streams that were offshoots of the Krzna River. Here and there farmhouses stood, dotted across the landscape. The nearest buildings were half-a-mile further east where a pasture dropped gently down to a stream. On the far side of the stream, and built on a slight rise, stood a farm and a cluster of outbuildings. But between that farmhouse and the edge of the airstrip where Major Nowak stood trembling there was just a ragged waist-high stone wall and rickety old wooden gate that delineated two fields.

Major Nowak climbed down from the Ford and flung his binoculars up to his eyes. There, on the far horizon and obscured by a cloud of dust, he could see enemy armor. They were perhaps still six kilometers away, but closing at high speed.

"Mother of all things Holy," he gasped when he saw the phalanx of enemy tanks athwart the distant skyline. He was staring at defeat; staring at imminent disaster. He knew he should give orders, knew too that his men were looking to him for calm, composed leadership. But in that moment of cringing terror, he was left utterly speechless.

"Should we dig trenches, sir?" the Captain in command of the infantry Company stood red-faced and fidgeting with alarm. "What about the trucks? Shall I have them moved back to the train station?"

Nowak stared numbly at the officer as though he had never seen him before, his mind a turmoil. He opened his mouth to speak at last, but the words were smothered by the sudden fury of an artillery round that streaked across the sky and landed amongst a grove of trees a hundred yards short of the airstrip. The Polish infantry scattered and threw themselves down into the long grass. The round exploded in a vast eruption of flames and smoke and the ground heaved up, flailing debris and shrapnel in every direction. One soldier shrieked in pain and fell onto his back, his legs thrashing, but he was the only victim.

A dozen more artillery rounds followed a few seconds after the first crashing explosion, each one falling amongst the Polish troops, the echo of them slamming monstrously against the sky. The air quivered with the force of each explosion and filled with thick boiling smoke. Someone in the choking confusion shouted for the troops to retreat. The voice came loud and terrified and the cry was picked up by others and repeated. Major Nowak saw shapes in the haze running back through the veil of smoke… and he ran with them, his feet pounding in the grass as panic spread like contagion.

Then suddenly another voice was shouting; a savage, demanding roar that stopped men dead in their tracks and forced others to falter, shamefaced.

"Stand your ground!" Colonel Armstrong bellowed above the shriek and hammer of incoming enemy shells. "Make sure you're loaded and form up at the eastern end of the airstrip." Behind him followed the sound of grinding, clattering steel tracks. Abrams tanks emerged from out of the haze. Lieutenant Jim Grimsby stood upright in his commander's turret hatch, leading the four vehicles of White Platoon.

Grimsby's Abrams, and his wingman from Alpha Section, White Two, had been the two tanks Armstrong had held in reserve. White Four and White Three had been pulled away from the defense of the eastern bridge and ordered to the airstrip for a suicidal battle against the approaching Belarusian force.

The sight of the American MBTs steadied the routing Polish infantry. "Major Nowak!" Armstrong put fury into his voice. The Polish officer appeared from behind a writhing twist of white smoke.

"Colonel?"

"Lead your men forward at the double. I want them in the grass east of here ready to receive enemy infantry in thirty seconds."

"Colonel?" Nowak's face went white with shock.

"Do it!" Armstrong had no time for politics or diplomacy. The defense of Biala Podlaska hung by a thread.

Pounding footsteps sounded from the city's outskirts and Armstrong turned to see a Company of his paratroopers running in orderly training-ground ranks, being led by Charlie Mott. The Sky Soldiers had been drawn from the defense of the riverbank and were sprinting through the dissipating smoke grim-faced and resolved. They went past the Colonel in a rush of bodies, shouldering their weapons as they dashed forward to bolster the Polish ranks.

"It's not much," Armstrong stared at the backs of the paratroopers as they passed him.

"It'll have to do," Mott shrugged. "Two hundred men and four tanks are all we have to spare."

The Belarusian artillery fire ended and the smoke began to drift away to the south so that when Armstrong peered at the far horizon, he saw the enemy attack taking shape. He counted over thirty T-72s in the vanguard of the formation with twice as many APCs following several hundred yards behind. Lieutenant Grimsby led his tanks forward into the field east of the airstrip. The four Abrams raced across the ground, their steel tracks churning deep furrows in the soft earth until they reached the distant farmhouse and its outbuildings.

The first blows in the fight to save the city would be long-range punches.

*

The Belarusian T-72 tanks disappeared into a shallow fold of ground four kilometers to the east of the airstrip. When they climbed the near slope and reemerged into sight again, they had split into three Company-sized prongs, each phalanx consisting of a dozen MBTs. The trailing Battalions of APCs, too, had split, with one column following the tanks to the south and the other shadowing the tanks to the north.

Lieutenant Grimsby's Abrams Platoon reached the farm and the four vehicles parked hull-down behind buildings, taking up hasty defensive positions.

Grimsby's strategy was to engage the Belarusian armor at distance and keep them at arm's length where the Abrams had a decided advantage in killing power, ammunition quality, and armor protection. At anything beyond a thousand yards the American tanker reckoned his MBTs were safe from front-on enemy gunfire. The trick was to throw his punches before the Belarusians could close or outflank his position, and then to hastily fall back to keep the range long.

The Belarusians knew they were outgunned. They were attacking in older-model T-72s from the Soviet era that lacked the long-range killing power of the Abrams. They needed to get close and fire at the vulnerable side and rear armor of their enemy – but to do so required a headlong charge into the waiting jaws of death, or to come to a stop in the open fields in order to fire their 9M119 Svir laser beam riding anti-tank missiles. The Belarusian tanks still operated the TPD-K1 sight-rangefinder, requiring the gunner to aim the cross-hairs of the sighting device at the target, fire the laser rangefinder with a finger control, and then manually input the information into the tank's analog ballistic computer. Besides range details, the computer also required manual input of ballistic and meteorological corrections. All these limitations, combined with a suspect gun stabilization system, meant fire-on-the-move was only accurate for the Belarusian T-72s, even at short ranges, when traveling on level ground and only then at pedestrian speeds.

"White…" Jim Grimsby paused for two heartbeats to allow each tank commander to select their targets before he barked urgently across the open net, "Top Hat! Top Hat! Fire!!"

The 'Top Hat' order was a term that American tankers used in a Platoon fire command to have all four tanks in the Platoon break their cover simultaneously and fire in unison at the threat they were engaging.

The tank commanders identified targets, the gunners lased the range, and the massive steel turrets turned. Then each Abrams rocked back on its suspension, the entire tank shaken by the recoil as leaping tongues of flame burst from the muzzles of the 120mm smoothbore guns.

White smoke blotted out the enemy.

The M829 APDSFS (Armor-Piercing Fin-Stabilized Discarding Sabot) rounds streaked down range and erupted in fireballs of boiling flame and billowing smoke. Two T-72s in the southern-most enemy phalanx were destroyed in the initial salvo and a third tank was struck on the front right-hand track, disabling the vehicle and stopping it dead. After a few seconds the turret hatch of the T-72 was flung open and a single crewman bailed out of the wreckage, enveloped in a volcanic pyre of black smoke.

The trailing Belarusian tanks slewed either side of the carnage, still charging ahead with grim determination, belatedly popping off smoke grenades to shroud their advance. Their formation broke apart as each individual tank commander navigated his own course to close the range. Tanks swerved left and right, zig-zagging to throw off the aim of the Abrams, and churning the lush green meadow to mud.

"Napierad!" the Belarusian Battalion commander shouted through his radio. "Advance!"

Behind the cover of the farmhouse buildings the Abrams tank crews worked with well-drilled frenzy.

Each commander peered at his CITV and they were overwhelmed by targets. They sought the closest, most dangerous enemy tanks and designated them for destruction.

"Designate tank. Load sabot!"

The loader concentrated on reloading a fresh M829 round into the breech; working with practiced efficiency. He thumped the ammunition door switch with his knee, forcing it to slide open, then reached for a sabot round. With the round cradled in both arms, he twisted at the waist to lay the munition on the stub-base of the open breech, lined it up, and drove it home with his bunched fist. The breech closed automatically; slamming shut like a pair of steel jaws. The loader instinctively crammed himself into a corner to avoid the wicked recoil of the breech, checked the 'safe-on' light by his left ear, and barked, "Up!" in a loud, urgent voice.

The process took just a few seconds.

The shout alerted the tank's gunner that a round was ready. He lased the target and locked on to the center mass of the enemy vehicle while the onboard computerized fire-control system made the necessary complex calculations.

"Identified!"

"Fire and adjust!" the commander gave the order to unleash fury.

"On the way!" the gunner squeezed the trigger.

The Abrams lurched back on its suspension and a pulsing shudder ran through the tank as the round scorched from the barrel at supersonic speed behind a leaping jet of fiery muzzle blast.

"White Two, eyes north!" Lieutenant Grimsby barked across the Platoon net. Grimsby had seen the far column of enemy tanks threatening to expose their position's flank and called out in warning.

The Sergeant commanding White Two searched the northern phalanx of T-72s, selected the lead tank, and thumbed the button on his commander's override handle. The tank's turret responded to the instruction, turning automatically towards the new target.

"Designate tank! Load sabot!"

"Up!" the tank's loader barked.

"Identified!" the gunner engaged the target and centered the sight reticle. He stabbed the laser button with his thumb. The range was eighteen hundred yards. The Abram's sophisticated fire control system performed its wizardry.

"Fire and adjust!"

The gunner thumbed the trigger. "On the way!"

The sabot round roared from the flaming barrel and streaked across the undulating ground like an arrow, striking the T-72 flush on the hull and tearing the Belarusian tank apart. It exploded into twisted chunks of black smoldering metal and a flash of orange flame, then began to burn like an inferno.

"Displace! Displace!" Grimsby gave the command for the Abrams tanks to fall back. White Three fired for a final time, striking a T-72 in the enemy's center column from just under seventeen hundred yards range. The depleted uranium penetrator dart struck the Belarusian vehicle's hull, burning through the layers of protective armor. The T-72 exploded in a massive eruption of flame and smoke and the sound of the vehicle being torn apart was like a sky-trembling thunderclap.

The four Abrams began to reverse from their positions, careful to keep their frontal hull armor facing the enemy, still firing on the move as they rolled down the gentle incline to the bottom of the rise and then crossed the stream. Two more enemy T-72s took debilitating hits to their tracks, stopping them dead and rendering them useless.

Colonel Armstrong saw the Abrams begin to withdraw and gave the command to his three two-man Javelin teams to open fire.

The teams were hidden behind gentle folds of ground north of the airstrip. They launched their Javelin missiles in 'Top Attack' mode and the weapons went streaking across the sky, climbing steeply through the smoke to a height of one hundred and fifty meters before beginning their terminal descent. The range was two thousand yards and the three missiles plunged down on their unsuspecting prey on thin feathers of dirty white smoke. They scored direct hits on three Belarusian BMP-2 troop carriers in the northern formation of vehicles and destroyed them, killing the crew and infantry inside in a flash of flame and a pyre of roiling black smoke.

"Reload!" the Javelins fired a second time, targeting the same formation and two more Belarusian armored personnel carriers were turned to twisted metal wreckage.

The Abrams reached the edge of the airstrip, still firing as they withdrew before the inexorable advance of the Belarusian tanks. The American tanks fell back between the infantry lines, popping smoke grenades to haze the battlefield.

The T-72s kept driving for the airstrip but the APCs in their shadow stopped suddenly around the farmhouse to disgorge their cargo of infantry. Hundreds of Belarusian soldiers spilled onto the rise. Some set up heavy machine guns in the farmhouse buildings while others quickly unloaded light field mortars. Most of the troops assembled behind their vehicles and then began to advance, coming down the slope and approaching the stream in a ragged line.

Colonel Armstrong peered through the thick whorls of smoke and saw the far ridge dotted with Belarusian APCs and trailing infantry, coming on quickly. The men were running down the gentle grassy slope to keep pace with their vehicles. The first of the BMP-2s splashed across the shallow stream and began to mount the reverse side of the slope.

"Sky Soldiers, follow me!" Armstrong dashed forward, running towards the low stone wall and its wooden gate, and he heard the enemy's machine guns open fire and hammer the air, and he recognized the grunts and panting breaths at his heels and he knew the Company of paratroopers were following him, and the far crest winked and flamed with tongues of enemy gunfire. A soldier close behind him gave an agonized gasp, and then finally Armstrong was at the wall, sheltered behind a waist-high barricade of stone, and more soldiers joined him, hunched and heaving for breath, frantically slapping fresh magazines into their M4 carbines and preparing to open fire.

Armstrong poked his head above the barricade and saw a scatter of Belarusian infantry splashing through the stream. Ahead of them the BMP-2's were huge steel monsters, their turrets turning, searching for targets.

"Fire!"

The company of Sky Soldiers rose from behind cover and a blast of hammering gunfire crashed down on the Belarusian attack. The roar of the volley drowned out the scream of the BMPs engines. Smoke filled the gentle hollow and for a moment hid the chaos and cruel slaughter.

"Fire!"

Armstrong fired again; not aiming, not carefully husbanding his ammunition, but instead flailing the horde of swarming Belarusians with a torrent of steel. The M4 in his hands juddered, and the enemy soldiers began to fall. A soldier stumbled into the long grass clutching at a gaping bloody wound in his chest. Another man cried out in agony – the sound as shrill and as high-pitched as a woman's voice, then staggered back, his eyes wide in horror, his lower leg sheeted with blood.

Armstrong's M4 clicked on an empty chamber and he cursed, reached for a fresh magazine, and ejected the empty mag all in the same motion. With his eyes locked on the enemy, watching them as they closed in a ragged wavering line, he twisted the firearm to the side so he could see the magazine well, then slapped the fresh thirty-round magazine into the slot and hit the bolt release button on the left side of the weapon which released the bolt, stripping the top round off the new magazine and seating it in the chamber, ready to be triggered. The reload took less than two seconds.

"Fire!"

Another torrent of lead was unleashed on the advancing Belarusians. An enemy soldier was thrown backwards, his arms flung wide and a scream of pain jammed in his throat.

His weapon fell from his lifeless fingers and he crumpled to the ground. A man nearby was hit three times in the chest. He collapsed face-first into the stream, his blood turning pink as the water washed it away.

The BMP-2s turned on the paratroopers with savage vengeance, hosing the stone wall with coaxial machine gun fire, smothering the battlefield with their thundering roar. A Corporal at the northern end of the barricade took two bullets to the head and was punched back into the grass, killed instantly. The man kneeling at the wall beside him was struck in the forearm and he reeled away from the fight with his free hand clamped over the wound, blood gushing through his fingers and his face twisted into a rictus of excruciating pain.

A Javelin missile streaked through the smoke and blew a BMP-2 apart, scattering twisted steel debris for hundreds of yards. Another BMP-2 took a missile hit broadside, yet remarkably did not explode. The vehicle ground to a halt and the three-man crew bailed out into the bullet torn hell of the battlefield where paratroopers cut them down.

One of the Abrams tanks emerged through the smoke, its massive 120mm gun firing, its muzzle-flash lighting up the grey gloom as it turned on the enemy APCs and savaged them. Four enemy armored personnel carriers were destroyed in less than a minute, turning the tide of the battle and forcing the ragged wave of Belarusian infantry to retreat. They turned and ran, their faces stricken, and the surviving BMPs followed, reversing back across the stream behind thick blooms of smoke.

Lieutenant Grimsby fired a final time at one of the retreating enemy APCs, then the monstrous Abrams turned on its steel treads and went surging north into the drifting haze.

Armstrong leaned against the wall, exhausted and dripping sweat. His eyes were red-raw, his face caked with dirt and covered in small bleeding cuts caused by stone fragments. He peered over the barricade at the terrible carnage. Off to his right, about a mile to the south, he could see enemy T-72 tanks withdrawing behind veils of white smoke, while to the north the pastures were littered with the dark smoking hulks of destroyed enemy vehicles and the field was ablaze with a dozen smoldering grassfires. His eyes drifted back to the ground before him, and his gaze wandered over the clumps of bodies that reached all the way down the slope to the stream.

The Belarusian infantry had been decimated in the firefight.

The corpses were piled in clumps where the fighting had been fiercest, their bodies thrown down in attitudes of terrible agony. The grass was a blood-soaked trampled ruin and the air reeked of death. Here and there men still writhed or groaned softly. A voice called out, pleading desperately for help, and then fell suddenly silent. A man crawled out from beneath a bloody corpse and retched painfully in the grass. His guts had been ripped open and dangled in thick purple ropes from the split-open pouch of his stomach. He sobbed, shuddered, and then collapsed face first and did not move again.

Flies swarmed over the stinking morass. They crawled into dead men's gaping mouths and across open sightless eyeballs. A Belarusian soldier laying in a crumpled heap by the banks of the stream fumbled for his gun with blood-slippery fingers. Both his legs had been severed at the knees by shrapnel when the BMP-2 he had been sheltering behind had taken a direct hit from a Javelin missile. He turned the weapon on himself and put a violent end to his life.

The paratroopers had escaped the firefight relatively unscathed. Six men had been killed and a handful wounded. One Sergeant who had been shot in the hip was doubled over in excruciating pain and a young specialist had been struck full in the face by shrapnel. He would most likely lose both his eyes to a surgeon's knife.

Karl Armstrong slid his helmet off and dragged his clawed fingers through his sweat-soaked hair. Charlie Mott emerged from the smoke at the northern end of the wall, his face ashen. He stared for a long moment, appalled by the gore and slaughter. He had served with distinction in Afghanistan and

Iraq, but neither he nor Armstrong had ever endured the horror of a battlefield like this.

"We can't hold," Armstrong announced. "The next time they attack they'll roll right over us."

Charlie Mott said nothing. The paratroopers quietly reloaded their M4's and the American wounded were evacuated west to where the trucks were waiting. Major Nowak strode forward from the grassy verge of the airstrip where his troops still lay prone in the grass. He stared in horror at the slaughtered enemy bodies and stifled the urge to vomit.

"We can't hold them if they attack again," Armstrong repeated his opinion to the Polish Major. "And if they launch another attack across one of the bridges right now?" he left the implied catastrophic consequences hanging in the air for a moment, then went on. "So, we have to evacuate west and find another place to fight them."

"Miedzyrzec Podlaski," Major Nowak said in a daze. "There is a major highway intersection northwest of the city. The Belarusians will need to seize it to secure their route to Warsaw."

Armstrong grunted. "How far?"

"Twenty… twenty-five kilometers," Nowak guessed. The two American Sky Soldiers looked at each other. Mott nodded.

"Okay," Armstrong's voice was an exhausted croak. He took one last long look across the battlefield. All four Abrams tanks had survived, the Polish infantry Company remained intact and the Paratroopers had escaped with only light casualties. It was all he could have hoped for, yet still he despaired.

Retreat?

The notion galled him.

He had been reluctantly compelled to defend Biala Podlaska and he had known from the outset that the terrain was wholly unsuitable. So now he would pick his own ground, and fight on his own terms… when they reached the crossroads at Miedzyrzec Podlaski.

*

The retreat began.

The first troops to be evacuated were the Polish contingent. The trucks lined up like a queue of New York taxis on the airstrip, and the Company that had defended the grass verge without ever firing a shot were driven away west.

Then, as the day began to darken towards dusk and the sky filled with lowering clouds, the men who had fought off the Belarusian infantry attack at the eastern bridge were evacuated in stages.

Karl Armstrong and Charlie Mott watched the trucks disappear into the distance with rising anxiety, aware that an attack by the Belarusians could spell disaster. They kept a wary eye on the eastern horizon and another on the sky, willing the onset of nightfall.

With the last Company of Polish troops went Janna Vidas, her cameraman, and two dozen obstinate civilians who had refused to flee the city the evening before. They loaded up their meager belongings onto the back of a truck and sat perched on the piles of their possessions as the vehicles carried them away to safety. Major Nowak saluted Armstrong solemnly then he and his staff departed in a fleet of Polish Army Ford Rangers. The Major had instructions to prepare the crossroads at Miedzyrzec Podlaski for defense, and to supervise the evacuation of locals from the small township that sat astride the vital intersection.

When only the American paratroopers and the Abrams tanks remained, Armstrong ordered the engineers to lay demolition charges east of the train station. If he had to surrender the city, he vowed the enemy would not seize the vital infrastructure intact.

The explosions would be a final obstinate gesture of defiance.

The paratroopers' contingent of Humvees under the command of Captain Roy and their M1297 A-GMV (Army – Ground Mobility Vehicles) assembled outside the train station. The injured were loaded aboard and driven into the sunset. Armstrong detailed a Platoon of troops to act as a rear guard at the airstrip and another to cover the western bridge, then ordered Charlie Mott to lead the rest of the Sky Soldiers west.

"I'd just as soon as stay," Mott protested reasonably.

"I'd rather have you here," Armstrong conceded. "But one of us has to get to Miedzyrzec Podlaski and take command."

Mott grunted, then cast a speculative eye at the cloud front building from the east. "Rain?"

Armstrong shook his head. "Charlie, we couldn't be that lucky," he grumbled. Rain would be the perfect cover for their exfil and might dissuade the Belarusians from launching another assault. He lifted his binoculars and carefully scanned the eastern skyline. Nightfall was perhaps another thirty minutes away but already the horizon was blurring into indistinct silhouettes. He thought he saw movement and he stood very still for a long time, like a hunting dog, his senses acutely alert. Dark shapes were moving in the darkening distance, and Armstrong intuitively tensed, suspecting the enemy were at last re-forming to attack the airstrip. He snatched for the radio clipped to his webbing belt and ordered the engineers still at the train station to blow the charges, then ordered the platoon of men entrenched at the western bridge to fall back to the train station for exfil.

"Double time it!"

He ended the call and took one last look around the verge of the airstrip. "Charlie, get your ass outa here," Armstrong's voice turned urgent. "If the enemy are gathering for another attack, then sure as shit they're going to suffocate the fuck out of us with artillery first. You wanna be somewhere else right now, brother."

Mott made for the train station to lead the last convoy west, so the only troops remaining in the city were the platoon defending the edge of the runway and Lieutenant Grimsby's seven tanks.

Armstrong put the binoculars back to his eyes. There was a distant rumble now, carried on the air, and sounding like a far-away stormfront. It could have been the noise made by approaching enemy tanks… or maybe it really would rain, he mused.

Then the far skyline flashed with a fiery red bloom of light and two seconds later the dark sky above the airstrip was shredded by the shriek of an incoming artillery shell.

"Incoming!" Armstrong cried.

The round landed well short of the concrete and exploded in fields to the north. It was the prelude to an attack. Armstrong glanced anxiously at his watch. He needed to buy the column of Humvees and M1297s time. They would only just now be pulling away from the train station, still weaving a course through the city's narrow streets westwards. Then three mighty explosions shook the dusk, each one spaced two seconds apart. They lit the sky like it was daylight and a horrendous thunder of sound cracked and echoed against the clouds. The explosions at the train station ripped up and buckled a mile of track, rendering the lines useless to the enemy, at least for the foreseeable future. It wasn't much of a triumph, Armstrong reckoned, but it was more than a petulant gesture, for it effectively denied the Belarusians a vital route of troop resupply.

"Fall back!" Armstrong cupped his hands to his mouth and shouted the order to the Platoon of troops lined along the verge of the airstrip. The enemy had the range and unless he conceded ground now, more men would die needlessly. He ordered the tanks and the soldiers to the far end of the concrete runway. The Platoon fell back in good order and the Abrams reversed. A dozen enemy artillery shells sped them on their way, landing amongst the grassy field the Americans had just surrendered. Swirling smoke melded with the night sky, pierced by stabbing fiery explosions. Shrapnel fizzed through the air and clattered against the steel hull of one of the Abrams tanks.

The Belarusian gun crews took to their work with a will, and the twilight sky filled with a hail of incoming artillery shells. The sound was a shrieking, hammering cacophony of explosions; a relentless ear-splitting maelstrom that quivered the air and gouged huge erupting craters from the earth. The sky became drenched with smoke and dust – and through that curtain of haze suddenly burst three T-72 tanks.

The concrete runway was over three kilometers long. Lieutenant Grimsby sighted the enemy tanks in his CITV and gave the order to fire on the lead vehicle. The sabot round blasted from the muzzle of the tank but flew two yards wide of its target. The T-72 fired back but the shot disappeared somewhere into the dark sky.

The T-72s broke left and right and behind them emerged more dark charging shapes.

"Mount up!" Colonel Armstrong ordered the paratroopers to clamber aboard the Abrams tanks.

The fight for Biala Podlaska was over.

Chapter 8:

It rained during the night so that when Karl Armstrong, the Platoon of paratroopers, and the seven remaining Abrams tanks finally arrived at the Miedzyrzec Podlaski intersection, the roads were glistening wet and the gutters running with overflow. The crossroads was a massive modern tangle of blacktop with an underpass running north-south and the raised overpass leading west to Warsaw. Offramps looped in a two-lane figure eight, connecting the main arterial roads that were lined with street lights and steel guard rails. Straddling the highway to Warsaw, a mile east of the overpass, was a cluster of homes and business that stood as dark silhouettes in the night.

Armstrong stopped in the middle of the blacktop and turned in a slow circle. He could see very little in the night. Far to the east there was a red glow on the skyline and he guessed it was Biala Podlaska being burned to the ground by the Belarusian Army. Closer – much closer – and away to the southeast, were the city lights of Miedzyrzec Podlaski with long lines of vehicle headlights streaming west.

The rain eased and a cruel, chill wind came hunting out of the south, shredding the clouds and allowing a slice of moonlight to show. Armstrong turned his back on the gusting breeze and saw the familiar figure of Charlie Mott striding towards him down the middle of the blacktop.

"What's the terrain like?" Armstrong gestured with a sweep of his hand.

"It's Poland," Mott shrugged, as if that explained all. "Flat and featureless in every direction for miles. Mainly fields and pasture with some groves of trees. No chance of the enemy surprising us."

Armstrong grunted. "Let's set up OPs five clicks to the south and five clicks to the north in case they try to outflank us, and I want a Company of Polish infantry attached to each OP."

"You really think the enemy will try the same trick they tried this afternoon?"

"No," Armstrong admitted. "But there's no other place for the Polish infantry. We've got ourselves a narrow battlefront – a town we can defend with our own men. The Polish are only going to get in the way, or, if we place them on the town's outskirts, become enemy target practice. We'll keep one Company here with the Humvees as a ready reserve."

Mott nodded and then frowned. "I'm not sure we have the authority to be ordering the Polish…"

"Aw, shit, Charlie. I don't have the time for the politics. Where's Nowak. I'll tell the man myself."

"He's in the town," Mott pointed east, "doing what you asked. He's making sure the civilians are evacuated."

"Good. That will keep him busy for an hour. In the meantime, we need to get comms established and an artillery park for the howitzers set up."

"Done and done," Mott was a better Executive Officer than he was a fighting man. "The howitzers are five miles down the road," he pointed west towards Warsaw, "and I already have comms established. HQ knows we had to retreat from Biala Podlaska and they know we're here, making a stand."

"Orders?"

"Hold at all costs until relieved. The rest of the Brigade should be in the air by dawn, and they have good open spaces for LZs to the west of us. Weather permitting, they should be here by 1200 hours."

Armstrong grunted and gnawed at his bottom lip. He wished he had arrived in daylight and had seen the battlefield first-hand. He turned again to the east and stared at the far-away glow on the skyline. Somewhere out there, in the dark night, the Belarusian Army was preparing for another attack that would most likely come at first light.

Charlie Mott interrupted his thoughts. "Do you really think it's wise to put both companies of our men in the town, Karl?" he prompted delicately. "The Belarusians are going to pound the place to rubble with artillery before they attack."

Armstrong shook his head, sure of his conviction. "No. They won't, Charlie. Because they don't have time," he turned and peered at the silhouettes of the dark buildings, and gestured as he spoke. "I figure it this way. The guy commanding the enemy launched his invasion force across the river at around midnight last night. He's almost twenty-four hours into his attack. He must have expected to be at the gates of Warsaw by now, preparing to assault the capital. But he's not, because we got in his way and held him up for almost a full day, screwing with his timetable. He's got to be unnerved, Charlie. He knows NATO will be trying to marshal troops to defend the capital, so he's under time pressure. Every minute he's held up is another minute NATO has to defend the capital, yeah?"

"Yeah," Mott nodded his head with slow comprehension.

"So, tomorrow morning he's only got one play he can run. He has to go to his running game; he has to rush us and overwhelm our positions as quickly as possible."

"So, no artillery barrage to soften us up?"

Armstrong smiled wryly. "There will be artillery," he predicted, "because he won't be able to help himself. It's right out of the Soviet manual. But he won't be able to pound the town to rubble before he sends his armor forward because he hasn't got the time."

The paratroopers and the Abrams tanks moved into the evacuated township after midnight and began knocking down walls to clear fields of fire and building defensive positions behind sandbags and brick walls. Janna Vidas and her cameraman scurried through the narrow streets filming. The paratroopers joked and flirted with the journalist and Vidas encouraged them with a teasing smile, stopping to accept a mug of coffee from a Corporal and pausing to chat with a group of engineers who were blocking an alleyway with piled furniture.

The reserve Company of Polish troops under Major Nowak's command sheltered in the cover of the highway underpass, huddled around Captain Roy's ten Humvees. The two Polish Companies attached to the Observation Posts trudged north and south, and spent a miserable night in the wet and shivering cold, digging ditches athwart the highway so that when dawn came, weak and watery through a brooding bank of ominous storm clouds, the small Allied force was, at last, ready and waiting tensely for the fresh hell that was about to be unleashed from the east.

*

The Sky Soldiers of the 173rd Airborne Brigade poured out across the vast tarmac at Vincenza, Italy, into the pre-dawn light. The men, weighed down by the burden of their combat equipment and made clumsy by the harnessed gear of their bulky parachutes, formed up into orderly long lines around eight Lockheed Martin C-130 Hercules aircraft that were queued along the length of the runway. Six massive McDonnell Douglas C-17A Globemaster IIIs were already in the sky heading north, laden with the Brigade's vehicles and light artillery pieces, and now the air across the tarmac was drenched and hazed with the stench of jet fuel.

The sound of the Globemaster IIIs lumbering north at low altitude and the roaring engines of the waiting Hercules was an assault on the ears; a relentless wave of whining, thundering, roaring noise that seemed to sweep over the airstrip in waves. The paratroopers entered the waiting aircraft via the huge loading ramps at the rear of the plane; sixty-four Sky Soldiers allocated to each aircraft, the men arranging themselves inside the cavernous cargo area in two 'sticks' on fold-down seats against the port and starboard fuselage. Quickly the cargo area filled with the mingled odours of sweat and the distinctive smell of the nylon harnesses and pack trays.

The men's faces were set and composed, but behind their eyes they were all on edge and pumped with adrenaline.

The five-man crews of each aircraft waited patiently for their cargo of paratroopers to board, and then the sound of each plane's four massive engines rose to a crescendo as, one-by-one, the C-130s taxied to the end of the runway and prepared to take off.

The huge ungainly beasts climbed into the dawn sky then banked north towards Poland, the scream of their monstrous engines echoing across the landscape and turning the air into a quivering, shimmering heat haze.

The American 173rd Airborne Brigade was on the move at last, and the Sky Soldiers were spoiling for a fight.

*

Karl Armstrong woke from a fitful sleep and went out into the pre-dawn light. The morning was eerily still, the landscape shrouded in mist, and the grass wet with dew. Overhead the sky was a blanket of dark grey storm clouds; an ominous forbidding portent of the day to come.

The Colonel stood quietly for a moment as around him the soldiers defending the township began to stir. Some men brewed water for coffee, others went yawning and scratching in search of a hot meal. A Corporal who had stood sentry duty through the short night perched himself on the front doorstep of a house, lit his first cigarette for the new day, and began meticulously stripping down and cleaning his M4. The men's uniforms were wet and clammy and the air was dank and smelled of smoke. A few soldiers sat with their heads close together around a small fire muttering quietly amongst themselves.

Armstrong crossed the street and climbed to the second story window of an apartment block. At an east-facing window he peered into the distance through a pair of binoculars. The highway was shrouded in tendrils of mist, but the fog could not disguise the stain of dark diesel exhaust in the distance. It stretched in a dirty grey smear across the skyline to announce the approach of the enemy.

Armstrong took a long moment to move through the empty rooms, peering through more windows to survey the ground to the north and south. It was exactly as Charlie Mott had described it; vast tracts of flat, featureless farmland that stretched in both directions towards a distant horizon of dense forest. He swarmed back down the stairs and strode towards the highway overpass, his steps brisk and purposeful.

There was work to be done and a battle to be won.

*

Colonel Stanyuta stood on the wooded crest of a low rise four miles to the east of the township and studied the terrain through his binoculars. He was in a foul, surly mood. He was unshaven, unwashed and unrested. Around him his senior command staff were all peering westward through the early morning mist.

"The town appears to be deserted," the Brigade Intelligence Officer ventured his opinion.

The morning was dull, the expanse of farm fields between the crest and the township hunched beneath a brooding storm-filled sky. A flock of birds took to flight in the grey drizzle, but it was the only movement on the vast empty landscape.

"The population probably evacuated last night," an Infantry Major flung the dregs of his coffee mug into the long grass and yawned. "By now every Pole within a hundred miles is probably fleeing towards Warsaw."

Stanyuta lowered the binoculars and shook his head. "The bastards are there," he contradicted his officers.

"Colonel?"

"They're there!" Stanyuta barked. "I can feel it. I know it – because if I was the American officer in command, it's exactly where I would choose to defend." He glanced at his watch, chafing with frustration and the pressure of a schedule that had already been torn up and re-drafted twice. The time constraint tortured him, but it did not make him reckless.

"Send a scout patrol to recce the township," he ordered. "And have observers ready. When the scout cars draw fire, the locations must be accurately identified for our artillery."

Twenty minutes later a Platoon of three BRDM-2 Amphibious Armored Scout cars appeared on the highway, driving towards the township in a column.

Colonel Armstrong was talking quietly with two paratroopers at the second-floor window of a building on the eastern edge of the town when the radio on his hip suddenly crackled to life.

"Six-Six, One-Four," an observer located in a church tower made the first report. "Three enemy scout cars on the highway about four clicks to the east and coming on fast."

Armstrong smiled wryly. The Belarusians were still faithfully following the old Soviet playbook. He ran up the stairs to the roof of the building and flung up his binoculars.
The scout cars were driving down the center of the blacktop, keeping good spacing between each vehicle. The commander of the lead BRDM-2 had his head out of his hatch and a pair of high-powered glasses to his eyes.

Armstrong reached for the radio.

"White One, Six-Six," Armstrong spoke quietly to Lieutenant Grimsby. "Are you ready?"

"Roger, Six-Six," the Lieutenant had the lead Belarusian scout car in his sights.

"Okay. It's your show from here."

Lieutenant Grimsby spoke across the Platoon net and put each tank on standby to fire smoke. "On my mark… three, two, one…smoke!"

The other three Platoon vehicles all fired smoke at the same instant, enveloping the fields immediately east of the town in a thick shroud of white haze with smoke grenades from their turret-mounted M250 launchers. The cloud bloomed dense and swirling, laying close to the ground in the still air.

"Designate PC!"

"Up!" Grimsby's loader barked

"Identified!" the gunner engaged the target.

"Fire and adjust!"

"On the way!"

'Crack!'

The wicked roar of the Abrams 120mm smoothbore gun shattered the tense silence. The sound of the booming retort slammed against the belly of the clouds and echoed like thunder. The lead scout car was blown to pieces by the hammer blow impact of the direct hit. The vehicle disintegrated in a sheet of lurid flames and a tower of black oily smoke. Twisted chunks of smoking debris were flung cartwheeling hundreds of feet into the air.

"Where the fuck did that come from?" Colonel Stanyuta gaped in shock. He was peering into the mesmerizing swirl of smoke that blanketed the outskirts of the township, utterly bewildered by the American misdirection.

The shot had come from Grimsby's tank positioned twenty-five hundred yards due *north* of the town where it had been hidden throughout the short night. The tank was concealed in a dense grove of woods. The savage roar of the shot rattled leaves from the trees and annihilated a thatch of dense shrubs.

The two following scout cars slammed to a sudden stop on the blacktop and then began desperately reversing, swerving onto the gravel shoulder of the highway, their big chunky tires kicking up clouds of dust to camouflage their retreat. It had no effect. Through his thermal sights, Lieutenant Grimsby calmly targeted each BRDM-2 in turn, destroying both in quick succession, leaving the highway east of the town littered with twisted black debris and the air trembling with the echo of each mighty gun blast.

With his ambush accomplished, Grimsby reached for a panel of three buttons on his CDU (Commander's Display Unit). A green button armed the tank's smoke grenades and the two red buttons fired off the devices in two salvos. Grimsby stabbed both red buttons and the woods he was concealed in became blotted out by a dense cloud of smoke.

"Displacing!" Grimsby had kept the Platoon net open. He had to exfil the woods and high-tail it back to the town, and for that he needed cover. The other three Platoon tanks fired off more blooming smoke grenades until the entire skyline was obscured in drifting banks of thick haze.

"Clever bastards," Colonel Stanyuta grunted sourly. He had watched the clinical execution of his scout patrol from the crest of the low rise. The misdirection of the smoke screen, he admitted grudgingly, had been a touch of tactical genius that he had not anticipated, rendering the observers he had posted utterly useless.

He set down the binoculars and turned to an artillery officer. The time for any attempt at finesse was over. "Hammer the bastards," he snapped. "Flatten the entire township."

*

Every Belarusian artillery piece opened fire.

The salvo came arching across the sky from beyond the far horizon, climbing up through the clouds and then plunging back down over the township in a screaming, shrieking torrent of steel and flame. The sound of the explosions became a relentless apocalyptic booming thunder that trembled the earth and turned the air between the narrow streets furnace-like.

The first enemy rounds landed around the western edges of the township and in the farm fields close to the overpass. One shell tore through a stand of trees on the verge of the highway, ripping down branches and shattering the tree-trunks. Another exploded flush on the roof of a convenience store, flattening the building and hurling shattered glass and debris hundreds of feet into the air. Smoke billowed in towering columns to merge with the low storm clouds. Fires broke out in several buildings and the flames spread until entire streets were an inferno. And still the Belarusian rounds rained down as the artillery found its range.

Four paratroopers huddled behind a waist-high wall of sandbags on a street corner were killed when a round tore through the building behind them. The brick and glass façade collapsed, crushing the soldiers. Three men died instantly but the fourth soldier was left trapped and bleeding beneath tons of debris. He screamed and sobbed, the sound of his shrieking cries haunting and pitiful, until he finally bled out.

Rocket salvos joined the artillery barrage, adding their own fearsome thunder of explosions to the relentless hammering rage. Armstrong saw a paratrooper blown off his feet by the nearby strike of a rocket and hurled backwards as if jerked by an invisible cord. The soldier hit the ground hard, writhing in agony from shrapnel wounds. The man cried out in pain and then his sobs became ghastly rattling groans.

"Medic!"

A medic who risked his own life to tend to the wounded paratrooper was himself killed by a subsequent rocket strike, both bodies immolated in a whooshing, searing fireball. Armstrong watched on aghast in helpless horror. The sickly obscene stench of burning flesh and oily black smoke-filled the Colonel's nostrils. He spat, then wiped his mouth with the back of his hand, and realized his fingers were trembling with shock.

The Belarusian artillery swept across the township like a passing thunderstorm. Lieutenant Grimsby's Abrams was shaken violently by two near misses, the explosions rattling the steel hull with a hail of shrapnel fragments and smothering the tank's position in a black roiling cloud of smoke. He waited until the storm of percussive detonations seemed to fade, and then spoke across the Platoon net.

"White, White One. REDCON status?"

The other three tanks in the Platoon checked in. All were undamaged. Grimsby switched comms to the Company net and repeated the call for a REDCON status to the surviving tanks of Blue Platoon. To the Lieutenant's relief all seven

Abrams had come through the inferno of fire and explosions unscathed. He cut comms because there were no orders to give and peered through the CITV.

Nothing moved on the far horizon.

The Belarusian artillery fire swept back over the township in another tide of thunderous fury. A church was destroyed by a rocket strike, a sprawl of low-rise apartment buildings were ground to rubble by a salvo of artillery rounds. A paratrooper hidden in the roof of a house had to be stretchered to safety by medics when the building he was defending took a direct hit. The impact of the explosion blew the soldier clean through the wall of the house and hurled him fifteen feet to the ground.

The barrage of artillery fire suddenly ceased, leaving the town a burning ruin blanketed in pyres of smoke. An eerie, uncertain stillness descended across the battlefield. The ceiling of storm clouds seemed to sink lower, trapping in the haze and the heat, and then a rain shower swept over the fields to the north, pushed along by a fitful breeze. The wind shredded the smoke to reveal a swarm of dark silhouettes on the eastern horizon.

The Belarusian armor, at last, was attacking.

*

The Belarusian artillery fired again, this time landing smoke rounds into the pastures and meadows east of the township to disguise the advance of the T-72s. The smoke bloomed grey haze across the landscape, but the breeze from the north shredded the top off the screen and tore ragged holes through the veil. Through those rents, grey hulking shapes emerged as the Belarusian tanks closed on the outskirts of the town.

Armstrong's CP was on the ground floor of a bank building in the heart of the town. He listened to the incoming reports from his observers and snatched for a radio.

"Stafford," he spoke to the Captain in command of the howitzers located five miles to the west. "Bring the pain, son.

Open up on the fields to the east of our location and give it everything you've got." He handed the radio off to an aide who relayed the grid coordinates and then strode out through the front door and stood on the main street. The eastern skyline was blotted out by white drifting smoke, but he could hear the menacing rumble of the approaching enemy tanks and then the distinctive sound of aircraft approaching, the thunder of jet engines wavering on the breeze. He cast a fraught look to the sky but the dark cloudbanks blotted out everything above a few hundred feet.

Fifteen seconds later two Belarusian Air Force MiG-29 'Fulcrum' multirole fighters came screaming out of the east and dropped below the ceiling of storm clouds as they approached the outskirts of the town.

The two sleek fighters flew line-abreast with five hundred yards separating their wingtips. They swooped low, flying at six hundred knots, and the sound was like a thunderous roar to signal the end of time. The air quivered, the shriek of their twin engines was terrifying in its menace. Directly over the heart of the town the two Belarusian fighters released a payload of KMGU-2 cluster munitions and Armstrong's world turned to an instant inferno-like apocalyptic hell.

Hundreds of submunitions exploded across the central district of the town, detonating indiscriminately on buildings, on street corners, in small grassy parks and in alleyways. The explosions shook the ground and the air was filled with thousands of shrapnel fragments that tore houses apart, obliterated abandoned cars and cut down unsuspecting paratroopers. The ground shook, the sky filled with black smoke and fiery flames mixed with spattered blood and gore.

In the blink of an eye the two 'Fulcrums' had flashed past. Climbing steeply and banking to the north, they punched through the ceiling of brooding clouds and disappeared, leaving the world behind them devastated and on fire.

Armstrong reeled in shock. From where he stood, he could see a half-dozen paratroopers down and dying. One man had his face slashed open, a twisted chunk of metal embedded in his forehead. He was on his back, dead, his arms and legs thrown wide with tufts of hair and the contents of his skull spattered across the sidewalk. Another man was in shock, screaming. His left arm had been severed by shrapnel above the elbow. His face was white and gaunt, his eyes huge with the horror. Blood gushed from the severed limb and splashed the wall he had been standing behind so that it looked like an abstract painter's nightmare. Another paratrooper tackled the hysterical man to the ground and smothered the sound of his shrieking while a medic pumped him full of morphine.

A dozen secondary explosions shook the ground and more fireballs bloomed from nearby streets. A paratrooper staggered through a wall of smoke dragging a shattered leg behind him. He brushed off those men who ran to his aid, his jaw clenched. "I'm okay," he sobbed, then dropped down dead in the gutter.

There was no time to absorb the overwhelming enormity of the devastation for a new sound suddenly filled the sky.

The American howitzers opened fire and added their own maniacal shriek to the maelstrom of smoke and chaos.

The first salvo from the howitzers landed short of the ridge to the east where the Belarusian command staff were observing the opening phase of the battle. The second salvo landed in the fields where the Belarusian T-72s were advancing. The task of the American cannoneers was to disrupt the enemy's formation; to force the tanks closing on the town to separate, stagger, break ranks or become isolated.

Lieutenant Jim Grimsby peered through the scrims of smoke and saw the grey ghosting shapes of enemy MBTs, still over three thousand yards away. The enemy tanks were close enough to engage, but not close enough to guarantee killing hits, and ammunition was precious. "Another thousand yards," he urged himself to patience. But in the meantime, there was still an opportunity to strike fear into the enemy tankers, and to give them a bitter taste of the turmoil that was awaiting them.

"White Four, begin sniper fire," Grimsby spoke across the net.

The gunner in White Four was the Company's acknowledged best shot.

Three times the tank's 120mm main gun roared its fury, and three times enemy tanks far in the distance were struck and destroyed by direct hits. One T-72 took a hit to its right front guard, destroying the track and immobilizing the monster. The two other tanks were both destroyed outright; turned into smoking ruins from over one and a half miles away.

The deadly sniper fire served to enhance the work of the American howitzers as the Belarusian tanks began to zigzag and swerve to throw off the American aim. Soon the phalanx of tanks had broken into ragged groups, some slowing and others veering north and south away from the highway. Smoke and dust obscured the battlefield so that the thin grey streaks of incoming Javelin missiles went almost unnoticed – until first one, and then a second T-72 suddenly blew apart and burst into flames. Both tanks had been struck by Javelin 'curve ball' shots that had climbed from their launchers into the clouds and then plunged back to earth, smashing through each vehicle's thin top armor and cracking them apart into thousands of jagged steel fragments.

Colonel Stanyuta stood on the smoke-obscured far crest with his binoculars to his eyes, fidgeting and cursing. The attack was losing cohesion, but that did not matter. The tanks were half-way across the open farm fields now, driving through thick smoke but still advancing. Blooms of fire stabbed through the haze and the sound of explosions became almost unending.

"Push on!" he urged under his breath. "Faster! Faster!"

In the distance he heard the sudden '*crack!*' of Abrams fire and he turned to his Operations Officer. "Get the APCs moving now! Our tanks can't enter the town without adequate infantry support."

The BMPs came racing along the highway in column formation and spilled off the blacktop, fanning out into the surrounding fields. The battlefield was a smoke-drenched chaos of explosions and flames. The armored personnel carriers formed quickly into Companies and dashed forward across the cratered ground.

From inside the turret of his tank, Jim Grimsby watched the enemy advance with rising foreboding.

"White One to White Platoon, open fire and keep the net open! Be ready to displace to your Alternate One positions on my word."

Colonel Armstrong had built his defense of the township in three concentric collapsible perimeters with alternate positions for each of the seven Abrams tanks. The outer perimeter defended the outskirts of the town where White Platoon's four Abrams were positioned and ready to open fire. The inner perimeter was two blocks to the west where most of the paratroopers waited in heavy cover and the three remaining Abrams of Blue Platoon were concealed. The core perimeter was centered on Armstrong's CP at the bank building; a fortified bastion of inner-city buildings that would serve as a place for a final defiant stand.

"Designate tank!" Grimsby called his first target. A T-72 at the northern end of the advance had appeared through a shredded swirl of smoke.

"Up!" the loader shouted as he hefted a sabot round into the open breech.

"Identified!" the gunner had just a moment to lock on to the enemy MBT before it was once again enveloped in haze. The range was nineteen hundred yards.

"Fire and adjust!"

"On the way!"

The shot struck the T-72 on the hull, but the direct hit deflected off the enemy tank's frontal turret armor in a flash of bright light and a billow of brown smoke.

"Re-engage!"

"Up!"

"Fire and kill the fucker!"

"On the way!" the gunner cried. The sabot round speared from the end of the barrel ahead of a forty-foot muzzle-blast of orange flame and flashed across the sky at supersonic speed. It smashed through the T-72's hull and the enemy tank erupted in volcanic flames.

"Target!"

All four Abrams scored hits in the first furious seconds and then the battle degenerated into a slug-fest with the Belarusians returning fire as the Abrams continued to thin the enemy's ranks.

White Three scored three consecutive hits on enemy tanks despite drawing fire from a handful of T-72s. The rounds crashed and thundered about the Abrams, collapsing the building it was hull-down behind but causing no damage to the vehicle other than destroying the bustle rack at the rear of the turret.

Inexorably, despite the lethal killing power of the Abrams, the Belarusian steel tide drew closer to the town's outskirts.

"White Three, White Four, fall back to Alternate One," Grimsby ordered the two tanks of Bravo Section to withdraw. "Move your asses! Go! Go! Go!"

The two Abrams reversed from their hull-down positions and vanished behind a handful of smoke grenades, and for a moment an eerie pall of silence seemed to descend the battlefield. As soon as the two tanks radioed they were at their first alternate position, Grimsby's Abrams and White Two began extricating themselves from cover.

The closest enemy tanks were within a thousand yards of the town's outskirts. As White Two spun on its tracks to reverse through a side alley, a T-72 appeared through the smoke haze. The enemy tank fired, striking the Abrams side-skirt of ARAT reactive armor tiles. The armor absorbed the lethal punch of the enemy tank's sabot round but could not prevent the two central roadwheels on the left side of the tank being destroyed. The Abrams lurched to a grinding halt in the middle of the alley, dead on its tracks. The T-72 fired again ten seconds later and the round deflected off the Abrams turret. The hatches of the American tank were flung open, and the four-man crew bailed out of the vehicle. A withering hail of coax machine gun fire killed the Abrams gunner and the tank commander and flung their broken bodies down into the dirt.

Grimsby's tank fired while reversing. The round disappeared into the wall of smoke ringing the town's outskirts. He reached his alternate position behind the corner of a building that gave a clear line of sight down the highway eastwards and gasped for breath. The interior of the tank stank of fumes and reeked of body odor. Somewhere nearby an explosion rocked the tank on its suspension, spraying it with a hail of rubble and debris, though whether it had been Belarusian artillery fire or a stray sabot round from a T-72, Grimsby could not tell. He peered at the CITV but his view through the thermal display was washed out white.

"Six-Six, White at first alternate position. White Two disabled and out of the fight," Grimsby reported to Armstrong. It took all his willpower to keep the panic churning in his guts from rising to the surface. During the firefight he had been a ruthless automaton, his every action governed by his training. Now, in the shell-shocked aftermath of the frenzy and with the enemy unsighted behind swirling smoke, he felt cornered. He could taste his fear, coppery and thick in the back of his throat, and he choked it down.

The Belarusian APCs reached the outskirts of the township and the infantry they carried spilled from their steel hulls and dashed forward into cover. The first buildings they encountered were the smoldering ruins of small homes and barns. Men armed with heavy machine guns and RPGs took up overwatch positions, and then the rest of the ground force began to advance along the narrow streets, supported by the T-72s that had survived the maniacal charge across the plain.

Karl Armstrong listened to the reports flooding in from his observers on the eastern outskirts of the town and turned grim-faced to Charlie Mott. "Tell Captain Roy to put his Humvees on standby. And tell Major Nowak to bring his Company of infantry forward. This is about to turn into the mother of all street-fights, and we'll need every man and gun we can get."

Chapter 9:

"That way!" Janna Vidas crouched low behind the rubble remains of a brick wall and pointed. 'Tosh' Kennedy nodded. Vidas went forward, across a street strewn with debris and Kennedy followed her. They could hear automatic weapons fire on the town's outskirts and they went running towards the sound of the guns. Overhead American howitzer shells were still arcing through the sky and exploding to the east, indispersed with the louder, closer cracks of occasional tank fire.

The air was thick with smoke and Vidas ran with a handkerchief knotted around her mouth and nose. She reached the far side of the street and peered anxiously around a corner. They were standing at the mouth of a narrow alley and in the distance, she could see a dozen Polish infantry kneeling and firing. She went down the alley with Kennedy at her shoulder.

"Start filming," Vidas ordered her cameraman, and pulled the handkerchief down around her neck. Her expression was tense and fraught. A stray bullet gouged a chunk out of the wall above her head and she flinched and cringed.

They emerged from the alley into a cauldron of smoke and fire; an amphitheater of roaring noise and slaughter. The Poles were men from Major Nowak's reserve Company who had been summoned from the underpass to join the fight for the town. They were defending a barricade of piled furniture and sandbags. On the opposite side of the street, Belarusian infantry were advancing through a maze of houses. Bullets flew like hail and there were crumpled dead bodies on the blood-drenched road between the two forces.

Vidas crawled closer to the fighting. Kennedy put down the camera, turned out his pockets searching for cigarettes, calmly lit one, then hoisted the camera back onto his shoulder and started filming the firefight. Vidas pointed to a building on the opposite corner of the road where a Belarusian machine gun was set up. Kennedy swiveled at the waist and zoomed in.

The firefight reached a crescendo. One of the Polish soldiers was shot in the shoulder. He reeled away from the sandbag barricade and threw down his weapon to clutch at the wound with his free hand. His face wrenched in agony, blood seeping through his fingers. He dropped to his knees then fell to the sidewalk on his back. The soldier who had been fighting at his side ducked down into cover and fumbled for a field dressing to staunch the wounded man's injury. A salvo of enemy bullets socked into the top layer of sandbags, kicking up gritty debris.

Two of the Polish soldiers still fighting at the barricade spoke urgently to each other, but Vidas could not understand the language. One of the soldiers nodded with a tight jerk of his head and then suddenly the Poles were moving backwards, stooped low to remain sheltered, but retreating down the alley. Soldiers seized the shoulders of the wounded man and dragged him bodily behind them. One of the Poles saw Vidas and Kennedy and blanched with shock. He shouted at them; his voice furious and urgent.

"Okay! Okay!" Vidas nodded obediently. The journalist and the cameraman followed the soldiers, running for their lives away from the fusillade of enemy fire.

When they reached the entrance to the alley, the soldiers dashed west along the street and were suddenly lost in the swirling smoke.

"Do we follow them?" Kennedy turned off the camera. Janna Vidas spun a full circle. They were utterly alone in the smoke. "Yeah, we –"

"Fuck!" Kennedy snarled.

"What?" Vidas' head snapped round. Kennedy's face looked aghast and awful.

"I left my passport behind," he said. "It was in one of my pockets. It's back at the barricade."

Vidas turned and peered down the long daunting alleyway. It was eerily silent. The shooting had stopped and the smoke lay in shredded drifts.

"I've got to go back for it," Kennedy said grimly. He handed the camera to Janna Vidas, then passed her a USB stick with footage he had recorded. "Be back in a jiffy."

He went forward, running at a crouch.

Vidas watched, suddenly feeling very alone and fearful. She held her breath until she saw Kennedy reach the far end of the alley and drop down to his knees in the rubble, searching for his passport. Then suddenly Vidas saw armed Belarusian soldiers appear. They surrounded Kennedy and thrust guns at the cameraman, shouting savage warnings.

Janna Vidas gaped in horror. A hand clamped over her mouth to stifle a scream as she looked on in chill, mute terror.

Kennedy rose slowly to his feet and raised his hands. One soldier thrust his weapon into Kennedy's stomach, and the Scotsman doubled over in pain. He sagged at the knees, his face swollen in agony. Then a third Belarusian soldier appeared, framed between the walls of the alley. He carried himself with the confidence and easy authority of an officer. He helped Kennedy to his feet and there was a brief exchange of words. The two armed soldiers relaxed and the man in charge smiled. Kennedy reached for his Press ID badge strung around his neck and handed it over. The Belarusian officer studied it closely. Vidas could see Kennedy's mouth moving but the words were lost by distance and the sound of rising gunfire from further to the east.

Vidas sensed everything hinged on the next few seconds. She stared, white-faced, her heart thumping in her chest. The Belarusian officer nodded his head finally and handed the Press ID back to the cameraman, then reached into his pocket and offered Kennedy a cigarette.

Vidas saw the tension go from the Scotsman's body. The Belarusian officer clapped him on the shoulder and smiled again. The cameraman turned and walked away, heading back down the alley. He took ten strides before the Belarusian officer calmly reached to his waist, pulled his sidearm from its holster, and shot 'Tosh' Kennedy in the back.

Vidas saw the Scotsman's face; an image frozen in time and seared forever in her memory. His expression was one of utter bewilderment. He stood for a second, took another staggering step, and then pain twisted his features and he staggered against the alley wall. His mouth gaped open, and his eyes were huge with shock. A bright splash of blood bloomed on the front of his shirt. The Belarusian officer fired a second time. The bullet struck Kennedy in the back of the head and killed him instantly.

Janna Vidas felt the earth lurch violently beneath her feet and a sudden roar of blood rushed in her ears. Her knees buckled and then she screamed in shrill horror.

The sound brought the Belarusian officer's head snapping up, alerted. He peered into the distance where Vidas stood frozen in the swirling smoke. He aimed and fired. The shot ricocheted off an alley wall. He fired a second time, the bullet passing so close to Vidas's distraught, horrified face that she felt buffeted by the wind of its passage. She threw down the camera and fled, sobbing hysterically with shock and terror.

*

"Fall back!" the Sergeant yelled the order and the Platoon of paratroopers defending a block of school buildings retreated in squads, withdrawing behind smoke.

They had been under mortar attack by Belarusian infantry for eight long minutes. The Lieutenant was dead and so were two others. Four men were wounded and had been carted to a casualty collection point in the center of town.

The remnants of the Platoon took up fresh positions in a complex of bomb-damaged low-rise apartment buildings, surrendering another three hundred yards to the advancing enemy.

"Higgins, put the SAW there!" the Sergeant pointed to a second-floor window that overlooked the ground they had just conceded. "Maynard, get on the radio to the CP. Let them know we're up against at least two Companies and we need help."

The men were bloodied, battered and near exhaustion. They had begun the battle on the eastern outskirts of the town, dug in and defending a row of run-down tenements. Now they were at the inner perimeter and giving up more ground as the Belarusians swarmed through the streets, attacking in relentless waves.

The Sergeant threw himself down beneath a smashed window and reloaded his M4. They were running low on ammunition. "When they come across that playing field, we give the bastards everything we've got and then we bug out to the far side of the road, understand?" He had to shout to make himself heard above the constant thrashing chatter of automatic weapons fire that carried on the breeze from every direction.

The men took up firing positions. The Belarusians brought up a BMP-2 and parked it amidst the nest of school buildings they had just seized. The turret on the armored personnel carrier turned and the evil black barrel centered on the apartment block the paratroopers were defending.

The vehicle's 30mm 2A42 autocannon opened fire, tearing chunks of concrete from the wall, shattering more windows and flinging broken glass across the rooms. The paratroopers hunched down, tucked themselves into tight balls, and endured the thundering fusillade while the Belarusian infantry surged forward.

When the autocannon finally ceased its murderous fury, the paratroopers rose into the cacophony of smoke and violence and opened fire. Maybe twenty enemy soldiers were flung down on the blacktop, killed in that vengeful fusillade. But by then the Belarusian infantry were across the street and the fight became a close-quarters melee against an overwhelming enemy force. Grenades exploded; soldiers screamed in agony. Automatic gunfire hammered the air.

Good men died.

Spattered blood – great gouts of blood – were splashed over the ground and across the walls. Smoke swirled thick and choking, and above it all rose the panicked screams and shouts, the cries of pain, the bitter curses, and the fearful confusion.

It was over in a matter of minutes. The paratroopers died hard, slaughtered to a man. Those who were wounded in the firefight were brutally dispatched by the Belarusians with a bullet to the head. Then the pockets of the dead Americans were rifled for cigarettes and money. One Belarusian took a knife to several of the bodies, cutting off the American's ears and stringing the bloody lumps of bleeding flesh to a cord hung from his webbing belt as gruesome trophies.

*

When Janna Vidas lurched through the front door of the bank building, the soldiers hunched over the map tables and seated around the communications equipment stopped in stunned shock.

The journalist's face was wretched, her eyes wild with grief.

"They killed him!" her voice cracked, dry with her horror. "The Belarusian soldiers murdered my cameraman. They shot him on the street!"

Charlie Mott swept to the door and propped the journalist up as her legs seemed to buckle beneath her. He guided her to a chair and she collapsed, her features ravaged and destroyed by anguish. Fresh tears spilled from her eyes and slid down her cheeks. They were tears of sadness, but also tears of savage anger. "They executed him!"

Karl Armstrong came from the back room and caught Mott's eye, a question and a frown in the Colonel's expression. "The Belarusians shot the CMM cameraman," he said. "He's dead."

Janna Vidas shook her head. "They murdered him!" her voice raged with strain and then she started to sob, dry convulsive gasps of heartache.

"Where did this happen?" Armstrong felt compassion for the woman's distress but his overriding concern was for the welfare of his soldiers. Janna Vidas described the alleyway and Charlie Mott found the location on the map. "That means the Polish in that sector are falling back…"

Another radio call came into the Command Post, this one from a Captain of paratroopers. The radio operator listened, his face grave, headphones clamped tight to his ears. He cut comms and relayed the message.

"Second Platoon has been overrun and wiped out by Belarusian infantry near a school," he gave the grid reference.

Armstrong reeled for a devastated moment, disbelief and chilling shock wrenching his features.

Over forty men and women killed…

His instinct was to give in to the grips of his grief; to spiral down into a dark pit of despair – but he forced himself to focus his concern on those soldiers still alive, still fighting. The time for sickening guilt, mourning, regrets, and the pangs of aching remorse would come after the battle was over. He lunged for the map. "Christ!" he recoiled. "They've punched a hole in our central perimeter. Who do we have to plug the gap?"

"We can throw another Platoon from the Polish Company forward…"

"Do it!" Armstrong snapped, then turned to one of the radio operators, the rising desperation raw in his tone. "Get HQ in Warsaw on the line, pronto. And put me through to Vincenza. We're on the verge of being overrun. If we don't get help in the next hour, there will be no one left here alive to reinforce."

*

Relentlessly, inexorably, the Belarusian infantry, supported on the streets by tanks and BMP-2s, ground the American paratroopers and Polish infantry down, pushing them back to towards the center of the town. Pockets of isolated paratroopers who fought on defiantly were targeted by mortar fire and then rushed and overwhelmed. Belarusian dead and dying littered the streets, the bodies piled high in bloody droves on corners and at the entrance to buildings where the paratroopers and Polish had fought to the last man, the last bullet.

The air stank of smoke and fresh blood. Machine gun fire hammered the sky, and the constant *'crump!'* of grenades across the urban battlefield was like the relentless beat of crashing drums. Two paratroopers were cut down in a merciless crossfire and killed. A handful of Polish troops were cornered in a building and surrounded by Belarusians. The Poles fought grimly until the enemy troops rushed the building behind a veil of smoke grenades. The Belarusian soldiers stormed through the building, guns blazing. The Polish officer was shot in the face and flung to the ground in a violent spatter of blood. Two of the infantrymen defending a ground-floor window were killed by a grenade that ripped one man's guts wide open and splashed the mangled rope cords of his intestines across the floor. The second man took the full force of the blast in his back as he cowered away from the explosion. Shrapnel flensed the flesh from his body, leaving the white broken bones of his ribs and spine exposed to the flies.

Two BMP-2s were destroyed by Javelin missiles on the town's main street, barricading the road with black mangled debris that burned like an inferno. A T-72 was obliterated by Lieutenant Grimsby's tank when the enemy MBT inadvertently surged across an intersection, directly across the path of the Abrams. The American tank crew reacted to the sudden target with lightning reflexes, destroying the enemy vehicle from less than two hundred yards away. The sabot round punched through the Belarusian tank's side armor, and the vehicle exploded in a vast fireball that ripped the turret clean off the T-72 and sent it cartwheeling fifty yards into the smoke-drenched sky.

"White, Blue, displace to Alternate Two positions," Grimsby made the grave decision reluctantly. Enemy tanks and APCs were swarming through the town's streets, increasing the fear that the Abrams could be outflanked and surrounded in the maze of urban sprawl.

"Repeat. Displace to alternate two positions!"

There was no alternate three.

They were withdrawing to the heart of the town from where they would make their final, defiant stand and all the tankers knew it.

At his Command Post, Armstrong overheard the comms from the Abrams. It was part of an endless stream of fragmented radio chatter, most of it broken by sporadic gunfire and the sound of explosions, voices thick with rising panic reporting in and competing over the top of each other.

"White One, give me a SITREP!" Armstrong leaned over a radio and keyed the mike.

"Falling back to alternate two!" Grimsby's voice crackled through a hiss of static. "Enemy T-72s on the main road, closing. APCs and troops approaching our perimeter…" the radio stayed hot for several seconds, but the only sounds through the speaker at the command post was a thunder of machine gun fire and an ear-splitting explosion. Armstrong threw down the mike in frustration. He raged around the room and then stopped suddenly, as if all the stuffing had been punched from him. "Charlie," he turned gravely to his XO. "Get Captain Roy on the radio. I want the Humvees and our GMVs here in twenty minutes to evacuate the wounded…"

The casualty collection point was a room at the back of the bank's premises. Armstrong went through the door to warn the medics that the fleet of Humvees were on their way. There were paratrooper and Polish wounded stretched out on desktops and laying in lines on the floor. The tiles were splashed and spattered with gore, blood-soaked gauze, and spilled urine. The cloying odor of antiseptic mixed with the stench of stale body sweat and the acrid scent of suffering.

In the midst of the team of medics knelt Janna Vidas. She was talking quietly to a paratrooper whose head was swathed in bandages. His eyes had been torn from his skull by shrapnel and his face left a bloody ruin. He was sobbing, calling quietly for his mother. The journalist had hold of the man's clammy sweating hand, and she was tending to him through his harrowing pain. Her eyes were vacant with sorrow as she saw Armstrong enter the room.

The Colonel flinched in recognition and nodded his head solemnly. Some dark shadow moved across his eyes. Then he stiffened and spoke urgently to a medic.

"Evac in twenty," Armstrong gruffed. "The Humvees are on their way. You need to get the wounded ready for transportation west."

He turned on his heel and strode back through the open door without another word. Major Nowak stood waiting in the comms room. The man's face was haggard and stained with spattered blood and grime.

"My men are falling back to the final perimeter," the Polish officer said. "A Platoon was overrun to the northeast of here but the rest of my Company managed to extract themselves before the enemy net could close. I have lost upwards of fifty men…" the Pole's eyes went to the map where he could see the paratroopers too were compressing their line and falling back against the relentless Belarusian assault.

An enemy mortar round landed in the street beyond the walls of the bank and then another round struck a shopfront on the far side of the road, collapsing the roof, crumbling a wall, and hurling debris and billowing dust across the blacktop. The wooden rafters caught fire and the building became an inferno. Another round landed on the sidewalk and a fragment of steel shrapnel tore through one of the bank's windows and struck the Polish Major in the throat, half-severing his head from his body and killing him instantly. He collapsed face-first onto the table and his bright blood spread in a pool across the map and drenched the floor.

"Christ!" Armstrong flinched in appalled horror. He lunged for Major Nowak but the body was limp and heavy in his arms. "Medic! Medic!"

There were spatters of blood on his uniform, splashes of it on the floor, and ropes of it gushing across the dead Major's body. The sickly-sweet stench of it caught in the back of Armstrong's nostrils and mingled with the dead body's sweaty stench. He laid the corpse out on the floor and covered the gruesomely ruined head with a scrap of cloth. The Colonel went to the rear doorway and called again for a medic, his feet moving without him realizing it; his body numb and reeling in shock.

Beyond the walls of the bank, the Belarusian mortar rounds continued to rain down, tolling like the infernal bells of doom.

*

In the sky southeast of Warsaw, the flotilla of American McDonnell Douglas C-17A Globemaster IIIs and Lockheed Martin C-130 Hercules were sinking lower to the horizon in preparation for the 173rd Airborne Brigade's jump into danger.

The Hercules were cruising at just five hundred feet AGL (Above Ground Level), banking steadily to line up on a course that would see them pass just three kilometers to the west of Miedzyrzec Podlaski. The paratroopers seated in rows along the outer walls of the fuselage heard the "Six minutes!" call and began to ready themselves.

The Hercules had been chosen as the troop transport for the drop because of its increased manoeuvrability and its ability to fly lower and slower over a DZ. The huge monstrous Globemasters, weighed down with the Brigade's ammunition, Humvees, M1297 A-GMVs, and howitzers, hung higher in the sky and slightly more to the east, maintaining an altitude closer to one thousand feet.

A paratrooper officer stood and strode between the rows of seated troops. "Get your game faces on, Sky Soldiers. We are dropping into a war zone so remember, this is strictly a hop and pop mission. Am. I. Clear?"

"Yes, sir!" over sixty voices chorused in reply.

All combat jumps were termed a 'hop and pop', meaning that when each paratrooper landed, their priority was to pop their releases and leave their chute, harness and lowering lines on the DZ, allowing them to prepare immediately to fight.

The Air Force Loadmasters raised open the paratroop doors on both sides of the C-130s, leaving a fold down step for the soldiers to stand on during egress. An aerodynamic shield immediately in front of the door swung open to reduce air blast.

"Six minutes!" the Jump Masters repeated. They got to their feet and went to their respective open doors. They handed their static lines to the assigned 'Safeties' at each exit to prevent the line being caught or accidentally activated while the men leaned out into the rushing blast of air to complete a three-sixty-degree safety check; inspecting the approaching drop zone, the aircraft's altitude and ensuring the DZ was clear of power line hazards. The sky was sullen and brooding with dark clouds.

The men seated against the fuselage waited, keyed up and pumped full of adrenaline and nervous energy. A water bottle was passed around between dry-mouthed soldiers and someone near the rear of the fuselage started singing an old *Credence Clearwater Revival* song. The men on either side took up the classic tune, their voices competing with the constant whine of the aircraft's huge engines as they sang about what they had heard through the grapevine…

Satisfied with their safety checks, the Jumpmasters leaned back into the plane and began to give the rest of their jump commands while the 'Safeties' inspected the paratroopers' parachute packs and static lines.

"Outboard personnel stand up!" the Jumpmasters gestured with their hands like in-flight air hostesses performing a commercial aircraft's mandatory safety instruction. The command was immediately repeated in chorus by the Sky Soldiers watching. They reached up and hooked their kit to the static line overhead.

"Check equipment!"

Starting from the rear of the long lines each paratrooper inspected the equipment of the man in front of him making sure helmets were secure, goggles were firmly in place and parachute kits were attached at every point.

When the flotilla of Hercules aircraft were just one minute out from the DZ, the Jumpmasters suddenly announced, "Stand in the door!" The men and women about to jump all shuffled forward as the jump lights near the door exits turned from red to green.

The two Jump Masters made eye contact across the fuselage and nodded.

"Go! Go! Go!"

The first paratrooper handed his static line off to the safety and then leaped out into the void, his body clawed away from the door by the savage slipstream and the frigid morning air. Training took over immediately once the paratrooper was clear of the aircraft; he clenched his feet and legs together, keeping his knees locked in place, and angled his toes toward the ground that was rushing up to meet him. He lowered his head, squeezed his chin tight against his chest, and counted down the seconds – just as he had done a hundred times in training.

Suddenly a violent jerking shock ran through his body, wrenching him out of free-fall, and he glanced overhead quickly to confirm that the static line had released the T-11 parachute from his pack.

The T-11 was an almost perfectly square parachute and had been designed to hold the weight of two fully combat-equipped paratroopers in the event of entanglement. Each man dropping from the sky was burdened by almost eighty pounds of combat gear which included a padded weapons container on the jumper's left side that held their personal weapons.

The air above the fields west of Miedzyrzec Podlaski filled with hundreds of blooming parachutes, strung in lines across the sky as each aircraft spilled its cargo of soldiers over the Drop Zone. At the same time, and further to the east from a higher altitude, the monstrous Globemasters began disgorging their precious cargo of heavy equipment beneath clusters of G-

14 and G-16 cargo chutes. Smaller G-11 chutes burst open above CDS (Containerised Drop System) equipment that included some of the Brigade's ammunition.

For miles and miles in every direction the sky became dotted with thousands of dark descending shapes dangling from their chutes, while the aircraft droned on, lumbering across the sky until they had cleared the area and began finally banking away to the south.

The first paratroopers out of each plane hit the ground and rolled, reflexively repeating their training drills, then sprang to their feet and thumped the quick-releases on their harnesses to get free of their chutes. They unhitched their rucksacks and other gear from their lowering lines, then dropped to their knees to unpack their weapons. The men were breathing hard, their movements urgent now they were in a war zone. Quickly they rucked up and moved out to their designated assembly points.

Brigade Commander, Colonel John 'The Duke' Pilgrim, parachuted lightly into a field of nettles to the west of the DZ and began barking orders the moment his boots hit the ground. He had seen the town in the distance while he had hung in the air; seen it shrouded in a pall of black burning smoke, and heard the fierce thunder of gunfire relentlessly hammering against the clouds.

"Major, I want comms with our boys in that town inside of five minutes, and I want vehicles ready to roll within twenty!"

Command staff scurried about the DZ, echoing 'The Duke's' orders. The Sky Soldiers moved with practiced, well-rehearsed efficiency. They knew time was of the essence, but they also knew they could only be an effective fighting force when organised and fully equipped. Each man went about his assigned tasks with a will as the seconds slipped by and the troops fighting three miles away slowly continued to die.

*

Karl Armstrong had no idea the rest of the 173rd Airborne Brigade had dropped to the west of Miedzyrzec Podlaski. He was fighting for his life; fighting for the lives of every man who had so far endured the relentless slaughter of the Belarusian guns.

The sky overhead was swollen with clouds and smothered in a thick choking smoke, and the air below the pall of haze was laced with automatic weapons fire and rumbling with the endless '*crump!*' of grenade and mortar explosions. Armstrong's entire world had telescoped down to just a few square blocks of blood-soaked ground and second-by-second survival.

The remaining paratroopers, Polish regulars and Abrams tanks had compressed to a ragged two-block wide perimeter to make their last defiant stand, and now they were under intense enemy fire. Belarusian artillery began pounding the verges of the stronghold and enemy infantry moved forward under overwatch support from BMP-2s. T-72s trundled along the rubble-strewn streets, firing HEAT rounds into any buildings where the Allied troops dared to counterfire.

Armstrong managed the battle from his CP but radio comms were rendered practically redundant. The Colonel need only stand outside on the cratered blacktop to see for himself evidence of the fighting in every direction, so close were the enemy to overwhelming his position. To the east, the north and the south, the foreground of town's buildings were set against a backdrop of black columns of smoke and leaping lurid flames.

Three of Captain Roy's Humvees made a heroic charge along narrow streets north of the CP and arrived at the collapsing Allied perimeter just in time to stave off a concerted Belarusian attack that would have overrun the Polish soldiers defending that sector. With their 50cal machine guns blazing, the trio of Humvees tore into the first wave of enemy troops as they marshalled in buildings on the far side of a street, and then savaged two BMP-2s that had been assigned to support the assault. Both enemy APCs were damaged and disabled under the hammering lash of the heavy machine guns, bursting into flames, and the infantry attack was mauled before it could gain momentum. The Humvees stayed on the street, themselves in great peril, for three long minutes to allow the Poles to reorganize their defenses and bring forward a handful of haggard reserves. Then the Humvees returned to the CP, the barrels of their HMGs still white-hot and their steel-floored interiors rattling full of spent shell casings. They parked on the blacktop outside the bank building to evacuate the wounded and then, fully laden with the dead and dying, they disappeared west along the highway.

Two more Humvees from the Light Troop Scout Platoon burst through the smoke and went barrelling due east. The vehicles were equipped with MK-19 grenade launchers. The limit of the Allied perimeter was marked by a barricade of mangled Belarusian BMP-2s that were still burning in the middle of the blacktop. The Humvees braked to a halt fifty yards short of the wreckage and fired their lethal munitions.

The MK-19 resembled a heavy machine gun. The operator opened fire, lobbing cartridge-shaped grenades that were belt-fed into the weapon. They disappeared east through the smoke and several seconds later a crescendo of *'crump!'* explosions and fresh billows of flame-stabbed smoke spread across the battlefront.

The vehicles reversed all the way back to the bank building where they too picked up a cargo of wounded soldiers for evacuation west. Armstrong watched the Humvees at work, his eyes on the vehicles but his ears attuned to the rise and fall of the battle's thundering noise all around him. At the far end of the street – from where the Humvees had just fired their grenades – he heard a sudden shout and his head snapped round in alarm.

A handful of paratroopers were running across the smoke-smeared blacktop, one of them shouldering a Javelin CLU. They disappeared into the front door of a bomb-runed building on the opposite side of the street and a moment later Armstrong heard a fierce firefight erupt. He went forward instinctively, his M4 in his hand and with no thought for his own safety.

When Armstrong reached the doorway to the building, he recoiled in shock. The entire west-facing wall of the shopfront had been torn away by enemy artillery fire, leaving nothing but crumbled rubble. Beyond the ruins he could see at least a Platoon of enemy troops and a hull-down BMP-2 in the grey haze. The infantry were a hundred yards away and closing. They moved forward in short dashes, working in pairs with one man covering the rush of his partner so they leapfrogged from cover to cover.

The handful of paratroopers took up hasty firing positions in the mess of broken bricks and shattered glass and opened fire. Armstrong threw himself down behind the remnants of a brick wall. A Belarusian soldier appeared behind a swirl of smoke, running bent double, and cutting diagonally across the front of the building towards a mound of debris. Armstrong tracked the man through his sights and fired. The Belarusian clapped his hands to his face and was thrown backwards into the dirt. The Javelin operator set the CLU to 'Direct Attack' mode and fired on the enemy armored personnel carrier just as the vehicle's turret turned and it prepared to open fire. The missile streaked across the sky in a blinding split-second flash and tore through the thin armored hull, blowing the vehicle apart and unseating the turret so that smoke and flames boiled from the cavernous rent.

"Come on! At the bastards!" the gruff voice of a paratrooper Sergeant snarled. He bounded to his feet, hurdled the wall of rubble, and there was a shout in his throat; a sound of fierce exultation without coherent meaning. The rest of the Sky Soldiers followed and Armstrong clambered to his feet and joined the suicidal charge.

He was shouting; screaming with anger and frustration and rage; in that moment utterly fearless. He fired at two enemy soldiers as he bounded forward, killing one man and missing the other. The survivor ducked down behind the corpse of one of his dead comrades and American bullets socked meatily into the dead body with a sound like an axe against a tree. The Belarusian returned fire, missed every single one of the charging paratroopers, and then died in a flash of searing white light and thunder as a flung grenade exploded at his side.

A paratrooper running at the Sergeant's shoulder shot at a kneeling enemy soldier at the exact same moment the other man fired. Both shooters went down. The paratrooper sagged at the knees, took three more heavy blundering steps, and then crumpled to the ground clutching at his groin, his hands sheeted in fresh blood.

As quickly as the charge had begun it was over. The Belarusians faded into the grey smoke and melted away, chased by a final chattering burst of machine gun fire.

Armstrong stood in the broken ruins, heaving for breath, his heart thumping like a drum in his chest and the shock of imminent danger only now starting to wash over him. His face was streaked with grime and cut through with runnels of sweat. There was spattered blood on his helmet and across the sleeve of his uniform – but it was not his blood. The paratroopers stood in a stunned small knot and stared bewildered at each other as though they had just witnessed a miracle. One of the men began to laugh; an involuntary nervous release of gut-churning tension and then they fell back to the bomb-ruined building dragging their wounded man with them.

*

When Karl Armstrong returned to the CP, Charlie Mott was standing in the threshold of the bank's door, made agitated by news he could barely suppress. "The 173rd are on the ground three miles west of us!" he blurted when Armstrong was still twenty paces from the bank.

The Colonel's step faltered and then a wave of relief washed over him. "Tell me you've got comms?"

"Yes! 'The Duke' has just been on the net. He's pushing forward towards our position right now. Our orders are to hold our ground!"

Karl Armstrong took a deep breath, bit his bottom lip and then turned away and stared east for a long numbed moment. He felt a choke of raw sentiment lodge like a lump in his chest and then tears scalded his eyes. He blinked them away. He had not cried since he was six years old. "Thank God," Armstrong husked under his breath with a rush of profound emotion. "Thank God…"

*

The cannoneers de-rigged and set to their howitzers while a fleet of airdropped unarmored GMVs ferried the Airborne Brigade's heavy weapons teams towards the highway underpass, from where they could lob mortar rounds into the enemy's positions. The airdropped Humvees rallied at the first infantry assembly point and began loading troops for transport to the battlefront. They reached the highway and barrelled through the outskirts in Company-sized elements, arriving on the war-torn streets outside the bank building. 'The Duke' and his XO were in the first vehicle, leaving his command staff at the DZ to supervise the rest of the Brigade's rapid deployment.

Colonel Pilgrim met Karl Armstrong on the steps of the bank and the two men shook hands and locked eyes. "A hard pounding?"

"They're determined, sir."

Pilgrim nodded. He turned in a full circle, his head tilted to the sky and seemed to sense the progress of the fighting. To the north he could hear heavy gunfire and see black plumes of smoke rising in the near distance. To the south the clamor of combat was subdued, and to the east the staccato of vicious firefights were being drowned out by the relentless whine and shriek of incoming artillery rounds, their explosions sending tremors up through the Colonel's boots.

"You still want to transfer to a fighting unit, Karl?" Pilgrim arched an enquiring eyebrow, subtly referencing Armstrong's repeated requests for a combat assignment.

"No, sir," Karl Armstrong said, despairing, and pale with desolation. "I thought I'd seen all the horror that war had to offer in the Middle East, but this is a new kind of fighting. It's savage. It's slaughter… and it exposes the very worst of mankind. I've witnessed enough of war's hell in the past two days. I've seen good friends and good soldiers killed for nothing but a few square yards of ground. I pray this is the last fight I am ever a part of."

Pilgrim nodded, then clapped Armstrong on the shoulder with a gentle, sympathetic smile. "Then let's make sure you finish your combat career with a victory."

He was a tall man, gangling in his movements, with a lantern jaw and eyes set deep beneath a heavy brow. He turned to the Captain commanding the paratroopers that were crammed into the parked Humvees and pointed. "Take your men north, Hicks. Reckon you'll find a fight about two hundred yards that way. Go and give the bastards hell."

Pilgrim strode into the bank building with Armstrong at his heels. The Colonel stopped in his stride to glance at the blood-spattered map on the table, silently noting the gore-streaked floor but saying nothing. The map matched his instincts; the paratroopers and the Poles had been pushed back to the center of town and were being hard pressed on three sides.

"The first thing we'll do is stabilize the perimeter," Pilgrim included Armstrong in his planning. "Once we can take the strain, we'll whistle up some A-10s and start to punch back. You still got tanks?"

"A half-dozen," Armstrong indicated their positions around the perimeter but was unsure those locations were still accurate.

"Javelins?"

"We're low on reloads."

Pilgrim nodded. "We can fix that."

*

For the next hour Brigade troops continued to pour into the western outskirts of the town, reinforcing beleaguered, exhausted men on the frontline and bolstering the fragile perimeter. Colonel Pilgrim worked the radios from the bank building and the front offices soon filled to overflowing with Brigade Command Staff and their equipment until there was barely room to move.

The airdropped howitzers finally deployed, joining with 'Chaos' Battery to add their throaty roar to the defense of the town. Mortars set up by the highway underpass received their first fire missions and began to pound Belarusian troops to the north where the fighting had been the bloodiest.

In the early afternoon the thunderstorm that had threatened to break since dawn finally unleashed mother nature's own hell. The clouds burst and the air turned grey with sheeting, pelting torrents of rain that swept over the ruined town, washing away blood, dousing fires that raged through ruined buildings, and cutting visibility to just a few yards.

The deluge overflowed the gutters, washed in great waterfalls from the rooftops, detonated on the blacktop, and pummelled the men hunched in foxholes and behind crumbled walls. It lasted for almost an hour as thunder rolled across the sky and jagged rents of lightning cracked and flashed and ripped the clouds apart. The day turned as dark as night and then a howling wind blew the storm away, leaving the scarred, muddied countryside in an eerie twilight.

The storm forced the Belarusians to break off their attacks and withdraw behind the distant ridge, but the Sky Soldiers never stopped. They splashed and sloshed, muddy and drenched and cursing and shivering through the torrential downpour, aware that every second of respite was precious.

When the second wave of Belarusian armor finally assembled and prepared itself to surge forward from out of the mist, the Americans had re-occupied the town's eastern outskirts and were ready, at last, to meet the enemy.

*

"Is this the best protection you can find, soldier?" 'The Duke' stopped during his inspection of the eastern outskirts of the town to talk to Jim Grimsby.

The tank commander leaned out of his Abrams turret and made a bleak face. "If I'm going to cover the highway approach, then yes, sir, it is," Grimsby nodded. His MBT was parked hull-down behind the corner of a bomb-ruined motel. From his firing position he had an unobstructed view of the blacktop all the way to the distant ridge from where the first Belarusian tanks would surely appear. The rubble wall only covered the lower front hull of the tank, leaving the armored upper hull and the entire turret exposed.

'The Duke' frowned. Dug in around the Abrams was a Platoon of his freshly arrived paratroopers, their uniforms still clean, their weapons unfired. With the Platoon were a couple of two-man Javelin teams squatted down in waist-high ditches and protected by a semi-circle of stacked sandbags.

"How much ammunition do you have?"

"Enough to put up a good fight for maybe twenty minutes, sir. After that we'll be throwing rocks," Lieutenant Grimsby said with frankness.

'The Duke' nodded gravely. "The rest of your boys?"

"Every one of my surviving tanks is low on ammo, sir. Most of what we had was needed to hold off the last armored attack."

The Airborne Brigade had airdropped tons of howitzer rounds, mortar shells, ammunition for the M4s, Javelin missile reloads, and thousands of rounds for the 50cal machine guns – but no one had thought to include a couple of crates of reload sabot rounds for the Abrams tanks.

In war it was always the little things – the minuscule oversights – that got men killed and lost battles. 'The Duke' wondered if this lapse would be a footnote in a military textbook one day, or something chiselled onto his tombstone.

Here lies Colonel John 'The Duke' Pilgrim – killed at the Battle of Miedzyrzec Podlaski because he forgot to airdrop tank sabot rounds to the battlefront.

The 'Duke' walked on; his head bowed as if deep in thought. Karl Armstrong ghosted to the Colonel's shoulder. Armstrong had his eyes on the eastern horizon. The skyline was beginning to turn dirty with diesel exhaust; a prelude to the impending Belarusian attack.

The 'Duke' stopped to talk briefly with a handful of Polish regulars who were occupying a day-care center. The building had been long since evacuated and now very little of the house remained undamaged. There was blood splashed across the tiled floor from the previous wave of enemy attacks and the ground was strewn with thousands of empty shell casings. On one of the hole-punched walls someone – maybe a wounded Polish soldier injured in the first wave of fighting – had scrawled, *'Fuck off pigs of Belarus!'* with a fingertip dipped in blood.

The Poles were nervous; Pilgrim could see the anxiety and exhaustion in their haggard faces. He handed two men cigarettes, clapped another reassuringly on the shoulder and shared a ribald joke, then turned and headed back along the highway towards the bank building.

"They look like they've been through hell," he muttered out of the corner of his mouth to Armstrong.

"Yes, sir. And there's more pain on the way…"

The sky overhead filled with the howling shriek of incoming artillery rounds and a split-second later the first explosions erupted east of the town. The Belarusians were firing smoke to camouflage their imminent advance, but the snarling wind that had swept away the stormfront also worked to claw the smoke screen to pieces before it could properly form.

The Belarusians persisted for ten relentless minutes but finally abandoned their efforts in futile frustration. There was an interminable delay and then the artillery opened fire again, this time peppering the rain-muddied fields with high explosive rounds.

"They'll be coming now," Armstrong said with foreboding, his head turned, his gaze to the eastern sky that was streaked with grey contrails of smoke and filled with flashes of erupting explosions. There was nothing more he, or any of the command staff, could do. The time for inspections and pep-talks was ended.

Now the battle's outcome rested on the shoulders of the men and women on the front line.

*

Belarusian tanks appeared as dark squat silhouettes on the ridgeline, advancing beneath the umbrella of artillery fire. They swarmed down from the high ground and came surging across the chequerboard of muddy pastures, their steel tracks kicking up plumes of spattered grime in their wake.

Jim Grimsby dropped down inside the turret of his Abrams and watched the enemy advance through his CITV. The radio in his vehicle sparked to life as tanks along the mile-long perimeter reported in.

"White, Blue, all units hold fire," Grimsby cautioned over the Company net. "We wait until they're within three thousand yards. Lock onto your targets but hold for my word…"

The T-72s in the vanguard were coming on quickly, trying to close the range to the lethal American tanks as fast as possible. Those MBTs following in the second wave had a harder time in the mud-churned ground, losing speed and struggling to maintain good spacing.

Grimsby checked the range to a T-72 that was surging along the shoulder of the highway, trying to make himself less of a target by avoiding the blacktop. It didn't work.

Twenty-eight hundred yards…

"White, Blue…" Grimsby paused to give each surviving Abrams time to re-lase the range to their targets, "Top Hat! Top Hat! Fire!"

All six Abrams opened fire simultaneously and the boom from their unified muzzle blasts overwhelmed even the sound of incoming enemy artillery fire. The fiery flash from Grimsby's tank lit up the twilight gloom in vivid orange light as the massive barrel recoiled and the tank reeled back on its suspension.

The sabot round streaked downrange and struck the advancing T-72 flush on the turret. The round deflected with a savage *'whang!'* that sounded like the tolling of a mighty bell.

"Re-engage!" Grimsby snarled. He didn't have the ammunition to spare for second shots.

"Up!" the loader snapped, then squeezed himself into the corner of the turret.

"Fire!"

"On the way!" the gunner cried. This time the round struck the T-72 flush on the hull and tore through the enemy vehicle's armor. The vehicle exploded and the mangled metal ruins became engulfed in flames and smoke.

"Target!"

The Belarusian tankers responded by firing smoke grenades and beginning to zigzag. In the first furious seconds of the engagement four T-72s had been crushed to smoldering ruins; a cruel reminder of the American tank's superiority. The Belarusian formation broke apart into desperate fragments and the fields became a chaos of smoke and drifting dark shapes that surged and then disappeared again behind veils of haze.

The American howitzers opened fire, this time targeting the distant ridgeline and beyond where the Belarusian BMP-2s were loading their troops and forming into columns. The first salvo of HE rounds landed harmlessly on the crest, knocking down trees and gouging deep, dark scars from the earth but causing no damage. However, the proximity of the American fire sent a surge of panic through the Belarusians who realized the fury about to be unleashed on them. The vehicle commanders shouted at the troops waiting to board and pandemonium broke out. Into that milling confusion, the second salvo of howitzer rounds landed, causing untold mayhem and slaughter.

Until this moment the American howitzers had been largely deprived of suitable targets. Now, in a few furious moments, they justified their value. Enemy infantry caught in the open were obliterated by explosions and shredded by shrapnel. The parked BMP-2s were cornered like rats in a barrel. Two vehicles collided, running down three blundering soldiers as they tried to make a desperate dash for the safety of the highway. Three more BMPs were disabled by close proximity explosions that punched straight through their flimsy steel armor and mangled engines.

Colonel Stanyuta watched from the ridgeline, helpless and bitter, as the third salvo of American howitzer rounds came arcing through the darkening sky on streaking tails of smoke, shrieking and whistling their menace.

He turned and peered east into the basin where his BMPs were still trying to marshal into formation and watched like a man living through a horrific nightmare as the rounds exploded and the killing began again. Men screamed; others were engulfed in flames. Broken bodies, and steel fragments torn from armored personnel carriers, went cartwheeling through the air. The field turned into a flaming cauldron; a furnace of savage death embroiled in black smoke and blood.

*

"I reckon they didn't figure on that," 'The Duke' put down the binoculars and smiled with grim satisfaction. The eastern skyline was smudged with black smoke and drifting cloudbanks of dirt, and although he could not see the devastation wrought by the howitzers on the enemy's personnel carriers, the fact that the road remained free of advancing columns of mechanized infantry confirmed the effectiveness of the barrage.

It had been an elegant solution to a vexing problem. By pre-empting the enemy's mechanized infantry advance and eliminating the threat they posed before they could reach the outskirts of the town, the enemy's tanks had effectively been isolated and made dangerously vulnerable.

"Okay," the Colonel turned to his XO and nodded. "We've severed the snake in half. Let's finish the bastards off."

The radio network crackled to life as the orders were passed down the chain of command. *"Open fire! Kill the T-72s!"*

"Designate tank. Load sabot!" Jim Grimsby watched a T-72 swerve left and then turn sharply to the right, bulldozing its way through a distant fence.

"Up!" the loader said in a loud, urgent voice.

"Identified!" the gunner snarled. So far, Grimsby's Abrams had killed three enemy tanks and had, up until now, remained undamaged by enemy fire. That probably wouldn't last much longer. The Belarusian armor was closing faster than the American tanks could destroy them. In less than sixty seconds, the T-72s would be engaging them at closer range where the Abrams no longer had a substantial advantage -- especially in the chaotic maze of a rubble-ravaged urban environment.

"Fire and adjust!" Grimsby gave the order.

"On the way!" the gunner squeezed the trigger.

The Abrams jolted as the sabot round exploded from the barrel. The breech slammed back inside the turret and the interior of the tank filled with the pungent stench of fumes. Grimsby was already searching his CITV for another enemy tank when the gunner confirmed the hit.

"Target!"

From within the sprawl of buildings, the two-man Javelin teams went to work, adding their own awesome fury to the clamor.

Every team had a handful of reloads and an abundance of targets to fire upon. One by one, the missiles flashed from their CLUs and went tearing up into the sky on wavering tails of smoke. The 'Top Attack' mode used by Javelin operators at ranges above a few hundred yards was specifically designed to take advantage of an enemy main battle tank's weakest point; its top armor. Conventional tanks carried their thickest armor protection on the front of the hull and the turret, but for years the vehicle's top armor had been neglected due to a lack of viable threats. The innovators of the American FGM-148 Javelin sought to maximize that vulnerability by designing an anti-tank missile that would launch into the sky, gain altitude, and then home in on an enemy tank from above where its impact could cause the most devastation.

The Javelins rained down when they reached the terminal phase of their trajectory and the destruction they wrought was apocalyptic.

Four T-72s suddenly exploded without warning, each one smashed apart by direct hits. One tank exploded outwards. Another blew apart with such force that the massive turret was wrenched from the hull and flung into the muddy field nearby. The other T-72s simply stopped, dead on their tracks, and began to 'brew up'. Flames boiled from sprung hatches and then black oily smoke billowed into the sky. A single Belarusian tank crewman miraculously survived the Javelin attacks. He scrambled out through his tank's narrow driver's hatch and fell to the ground, his uniform covered in licking flames. He staggered as the fire engulfed him. His ghastly screams of pain were cut short by the wicked retort of a rifle bullet fired from a paratrooper.

Colonel Stanyuta didn't need the powerful magnification of his binoculars to see and sense the tank attack was losing momentum. A dozen T-72s had already been destroyed and the first wave of vehicles were only now reaching the outskirts of the town. "Get our AFVs forward!" he turned and roared at his operations officer.

The man turned, helpless. The basin east of the ridge was a wrecker's yard of blackened, burning steel carcasses and hundreds of dead or dying infantry.

"What AFVs, my Colonel?" the officer gestured lamely. Smoke still drifted over the carnage but not enough to disguise the wretched toll the American howitzers had taken. As many as twenty armored fighting vehicles were scorched, twisted hulks, or still burning fiercely. Amidst the vehicles dazed and wounded soldiers milled, some stumbling over the dead, others weeping, or sobbing inconsolably. "Our mechanized infantry has been devastated."

"Then send what is left!" Stanyuta roared, blithely not bothering to acknowledge the disaster by giving it his attention. "Send everything we still have forward immediately!"

*

The first of the BMP-2s broke from behind the cover of the ridge, using the highway to race westward. They came in no formation, but rather as a ragged horde, each driver steering his own course towards the town's outskirts. As they closed within range, some BMPs veered nervously to the south, hoping to avoid the attention of the Abrams and Javelins. Others ploughed into the mud-churned meadows, following the trails carved into the boggy earth by their tanks and using the advance of the T-72s to shield them.

Only the foolhardy who sought glory and medals pelted at high speed straight along the blacktop.

Despite the savage mauling of the American howitzers, over fifty BMPs launched the suicidal charge. In the cramped hull of each vehicle were a handful of men; three full Companies in total. But they were being delivered to the battlefront piecemeal rather than in a solid wave of soldiers. Some BMPs slewed to a halt two hundred yards short of the town's outskirts and the men stepped out into a no-man's land that was criss-crossed with snarling machine gun fire. The vehicles to the south of the road charged to within fifty yards of a warehouse complex before they skidded broadside to shelter their cargo of troops from enemy gunfire. The BMPs held their positions just long enough for their rear doors swung open and the men inside to disembark.

The BMPs surging along the blacktop never closed within a thousand yards of the town's outskirts. Lieutenant Grimsby's Abrams destroyed the first two vehicles and then exploded three more of the troop carriers as the survivors hastily retreated east.

The AFVs to the north floundered in the mud but pushed on remorselessly. Some vehicles continued as far as the town's broken fence line before unloading their infantry. Other, more timid and terrified commanders, ordered their drivers to dump the troops contained in their steel hulls into the middle of the pasture, still hundreds of yards from cover, rather than risk their vehicles to the whip-crack of enemy Abrams fire.

It was a disaster.

Belarusian tanks, AFVs and troops all milled in disarray, unable to push forward into the teeth of the American defenses, and unable to fall back to safety. One by one the T-72s began to erupt in smoke and flames as the last of the sabot rounds carried by the Abrams tanks tore them to pieces. Two T-72s managed to burst through a barricaded alley to the north of the town but they were ambushed by Javelin teams and both vehicles disabled. The crews climbed from the smoking ruins of their tanks and threw up their hands in surrender.

The enemy infantry south of the highway mounted a concerted attack, reaching an intersection and defending the ground they won against three determined paratrooper counterattacks. Finally, the Sky Soldiers withdrew two streets to the west in frustration and called in a barrage of mortar fire that pounded the resolve from the enemy and forced them to fall back all the way to the edge of town.

In the north a fierce firefight erupted between paratroopers and advance elements of enemy infantry. The Belarusians charged under the umbrella of covering fire from two BMPs. The troops reached the town's first row of buildings before being heroically driven back by a Platoon of determined Sky Soldiers. In the blaze of spitting gunfire, a paratrooper Sergeant was shot through the eye and killed instantly. The woman in the trench beside the Sergeant had her ear shot away but continued to fight on while the blood splashed down her neck and soaked her shoulder.

'The Duke' watched the battle unfolding from an OP in a church, his pulse never quickening, his heart rate never climbing above fifty beats per minute. He could see the enemy tanks paused on the town's perimeter, waiting for infantry support before they dared to advance, and he could see the infantry, ragged and floundering, unable to be delivered to the battlefront as an effective force. Slowly, the enemy assault was losing momentum and breaking into isolated pockets of defiance.

"Now," he said casually from the corner of his mouth to the JTAC (Joint Terminal Attack Controller). "Contact Buffalo Flight…"

The ROMAD was the junior member in the TACP (Tactical Air Control Party). He connected comms to a pair of USAF F-16 fighters flying an XCAS mission. The fighters were the dedicated aircraft for on-call close air support east of Warsaw. The Vipers had been orbiting the sky at twenty-two thousand feet waiting for a CAS (Close Air Support) situation…

The JTAC gave the Vipers the details of the mission and the two F-16s banked east and accelerated. The fighters were not the best suited combat aircraft for CAS missions, but they were more than adequate for the task Colonel John Pilgrim had carefully planned.

The Vipers came in from the east, cleared hot, flying at ten thousand feet to negate most of the potential enemy ground fire. They were each carrying GBU-38 five-hundred-pound JDAMs (Joint Direct Attack Munitions) beneath their wings and a full load of ammunition for their M61A1 six-barrel Gatling guns. Four miles east of the battlefield they banked hard to the right, swinging momentarily away from the fighting in order to make a south-to-north approach.

The lead aircraft swept over the muddy meadows, dropping its payload of GBU-38s amidst the enemy's milling armor north of the highway. The earth trembled and the air seemed to shatter as the bombs detonated into massive flame-stabbed billows of black boiling smoke that bloomed four hundred feet into the sky. Five T-72s were destroyed by the monstrous explosions and two BMP-2s were then engulfed in the flames. One of the armored fighting vehicles caught fire and exploded. The other burned until all that remained was a twisted black metal skeleton.

Six seconds later the trailing Viper dropped its bombs five hundred yards further to the north of the initial explosions. The enemy vehicles destroyed in the first bombing run were still burning furiously. The pilot used their flaming wreckage as a marker. Another T-72 disappeared beneath the massive eruption of flames and smoke.

The sudden air attack was enough to stun the remaining enemy tanks and AFVs. When the two fighter jets circled sharply and lined up for a return strafing run from the north, the attackers' last shreds of resolve crumbled. Their reluctance to press home the assault suddenly turned into a fear-filled rout.

The Vipers descended until they were howling across the sky at low altitude, sweeping over the battlefield with their Gatling guns blazing. Beneath the nose of the lead jet three more BMP-2's erupted into flames as it swooped by. The trailing Viper targeted a Company of Belarusian infantry to the south of the highway, the Gatling gun mounted within the fuselage on the left side of the cockpit spitting flame and making the jet's airframe judder as the plane streaked overhead. The ground churned to a boiling mist and half the enemy soldiers were flung down and horribly mutilated by the hammer blow impact of the 20mm cannon's shells. The air attack was over in less than five minutes but the shattering impact of the Viper strike utterly broke the resolve of the Belarusians.

Colonel Pilgrim and Karl Armstrong watched the two Vipers disappear to the southeast and then turned back to survey the aftermath. The damage the fighters had inflicted on the Belarusian armored attack was appalling. The battlefield was littered with burning, blackened wrecks, each destroyed vehicle marked by a rising column of smoke. Dead bodies lay scattered across the meadow and to the south, where the Company of enemy soldiers had been savaged, the corpses were piled high into bloody ruined mounds.

Colonel Pilgrim put down his glasses. Binoculars were no longer necessary. The enemy were retreating; falling back in broken panic. 'The Duke' shook his head gravely. "It's cruel work, Karl," he gave Armstrong a strained flicker of a smile that looked very much like a grimace. "And it's gruesome. It's enough to make a grown man puke. But if we don't do it, who will deny these ruthless bastards the world?"

Epilogue:

'Tosh' Kennedy's expensive CMM camera had been destroyed.

Left abandoned on the rubble-littered street in front of the alley where he was murdered, it had been crushed beneath the steel track of a T-72.

So, Janna Vidas was making do with the camera built into her cell phone to record her latest report.

The phone was propped up against a stack of fuel-filled jerry cans on the corner of a blood-soaked street, still strewn with crumpled bodies and sifted with lingering tendrils of smoke.

Vidas wore no makeup. She had been made haggard and haunted by all the horror she had witnessed. Her clothes were rumpled and spattered – but none of that mattered.

Only the message mattered.

"In my role as European correspondent for CMM over the past week, I've brought you coverage from the growing conflict in the Balkans and on the Polish border. I have tried to present balanced coverage by giving voice to the Russian-block countries and their claims that Allied provocation sparked the outbreak of fighting," Vidas spoke without cue cards, her gaze fixed directly at the camera. "I wanted viewers in America to see the Russians and their Belarusian allies not as evil, but as nations that have been harshly oppressed and stifled economically by Allied interference."

She paused for a moment, and her face somehow reflected a deeper level of personal anguish. She pressed her lips together as if to hold back a sob of grief.

"I was wrong," Vidas said. "The Russians and Belarusians *are* evil. They are an evil empire, run by evil men and served by an evil army."

She let the words hang in the air for a moment, still staring directly at the camera so the viewers could see the rawness of her emotions.

"A few hours ago, my CMM cameraman, 'Tosh' Kennedy, was executed by a Belarusian Army officer just a few hundred yards from where I am now standing. We had been filming a firefight and 'Tosh' was intercepted by Belarusian troops. He showed his credentials to an officer, and then, as he was leaving the scene, the officer drew a pistol and shot my cameraman in the back. He then fired a second time, shooting 'Tosh' in the head. It was murder. It was an execution – and it was representative of the wicked merciless evil that the Allied nations are fighting."

She blinked several times and some of the stiffness melted from her shoulders. It seemed she would end the report, but then a final impassioned plea spilled from her lips and the look in her eyes became pleading.

"I've been asking why are American soldiers even fighting a war in Europe. Well, now I know. As a nation of people who cherish freedom above all other rights, Americans need to battle the sinister spread of Russian-block forces wherever they emerge. We don't need less American troops in Europe; we need more – more men, more tanks, more aircraft… until this cruel savage enemy is overwhelmed and – and wiped off the face of the earth forever…"

<u>Other titles in the collection:</u>

- 'Charge to Battle'
- 'Enemy in Sight'
- 'Viper Mission'
- 'Fort Suicide'
- 'The Killing Ground'
- 'Search and Destroy'
- 'Airborne Assault'
- 'Defiant to the Death'
- 'A Time for Heroes'

Facebook: https://www.facebook.com/NickRyanWW3
Website: https://www.worldwar3timeline.com

Acknowledgements:

The greatest thrill of writing, for me, is the opportunity to research the subject matter and to work with military, political and historical experts from around the world. I had a lot of help researching this book from the following groups and people. I am forever grateful for their willing enthusiasm and cooperation. Any remaining technical errors are mine.

Jill Blasy:

Jill has the editorial eye of an eagle! I trust Jill to read every manuscript, picking up typographical errors, missing commas, and for her general 'sense' of the book. Jill has been a great friend and a valuable part of my team for several years.

Jan Wade:

Jan is my Personal Assistant and an indispensable part of my team. She is a thoughtful, thorough, professional and persistent pleasure to work with. Chances are, if you're reading this book, it's due to Jan's engaging marketing and promotional efforts.

Kwuantae Santana-Rice:

Staff Sergeant Kwuantae 'Pedro' Santana-Rice spent four years in the Marines on the M198 and the M777 howitzer, and twelve years in the North Carolina National Guard on the M109A6/A7 self-propelled howitzer. He has deployed five times to war zones, including during Operation Iraqi Freedom, twice for Operation Inherent Resolve and twice during Operation Enduring Freedom. He is currently an active-service member of the Armed Forces.

Kwuantae was an invaluable resource for the scenes during the novel that featured the M777 howitzers, adding terrific touches of authentic detail to my writing to ensure the combat scenes were as realistic as possible.

Dale Simpson:

Dale is a retired Special Forces operator who has been helping me with the military aspects of my writing since I first put pen to paper. He is my first point of contact for military technical advice. Over the years that he has been saving me from stupid mistakes we've become firm friends. The authenticity of the action and combat sequences in this novel are due to Dale's diligence and willing cooperation.

During his distinguished military career, Dale served with the 82nd Airborne and was also the Jumpmaster in H Company, 121 Infantry Long Range Surveillance Company. In total, Dale served over seventeen years on Airborne status in the American Army.

Dion Walker Sr:

Sergeant First Class (Retired) Dion Walker Sr, served 21 proud years in the US Army with deployments during Operation Desert Shield/Storm, Operation Intrinsic Action and Operation Iraqi Freedom. For 17 years he was a tanker in several Armor Battalions and Cavalry Squadrons before spending 4 years as an MGS (Stryker Mobile Gun System) Platoon Sergeant in a Stryker Infantry Company.

Printed in Great Britain
by Amazon

60967390R00102